ALL THE WAY
FROM TEXAS

ALL THE WAY
FROM TEXAS

•

Carolyn Brown

AVALON BOOKS
NEW YORK

PRINTED IN THE UNITED STATES OF AMERICA
ON ACID-FREE PAPER
BY HADDON CRAFTSMEN, BLOOMSBURG, PENNSYLVANIA

With love to my son, Lemar.
For believing in me all these years,
this one's for you.

Chapter One

Molly Baker set her mouth in a firm line and her big, round blue eyes glittered with anger. It wasn't a big surprise that her fiancé, Darrin, didn't like the arrangement. Of all the people in the whole college, Carson Rhodes was the last one she would have picked to spend two weeks with. But Professor Johnson had made the selection, and it was written in stone for the whole world—or at least all of northeast Texas—to see. She could go with Carson and take one small baby step in the journalism world or she could stay home.

And she was going.

"Molly, you are not about to do this." Darrin barked the order like a drill sergeant. "You can just tell that lunatic professor you aren't interested and give him back the money. He can choose someone else tomorrow. There's a whole school full of women who aren't engaged who can go on the trip. No woman of mine is going to go chasing around half the United States with another man and me just stand by and take it."

"Oh, yes, I am going, Darrin Smith." Molly's nose was just inches from his as she leaned across the dining room table. "I'm twenty-three years old and I'm old enough to make up my own mind and take care of myself. And I'm not your woman."

"You're not if you walk out that door to run off on a lark like this." He pointed with a jerky motion toward the back door. "I'm not going to be the laughing stock of the whole country. Can't you just hear the men at the coffee shop? 'Where's your woman, Darrin? Out carousing with another man?' You can't tell me two people can spend two whole weeks together and nothing happen. I'm not stupid, you know. So you can choose right now. If you leave with that man the engagement is off," Darrin said, his voice raised.

"Then it's off." She took off the diamond ring he'd given her just last Christmas and laid it beside the sugar bowl in the middle of the table. "And you're crazy if you think I'm that kind of person. This is the opportunity of a lifetime. It goes along with my career choice, and there will always be times when I have to work with the male gender, Darrin. You've known that all along. If I get the right breaks I might fly to Africa or Australia some day with a whole planeload of men journalists. It doesn't mean I'd be going to kiss any of them. I'd be married to you and faithful."

"Over my dead body. You won't ever run all over the world like that. You're putting that professor and what he wants ahead of me?" Darrin drew his face into a frown. "Besides, I always thought after we were married this fall you'd give up all that crazy stuff and settle down right here on the ranch."

"You what?" Molly could scarcely believe her ears. She'd worked hard for five years on her degree in journalism and this was the last class. The final test of the final class to be exact. She and Carson Rhodes were leaving in two days on a photojournalism tour for two weeks, and Professor Johnson said their grade depended on what they brought home.

"I know you wanted your independence, and you'll have a degree to fall back on if you ever need it, Molly, but you don't have to work. You can stay at home and do what ranch women do. Help their husbands and have a family. If you just have to work at something before the children are born, you might work part-time at one of the local newspapers around here. Couple of days a week and you'd have a little free money. At least it would be something decent." Darrin didn't touch the ring.

"Writing obituaries and typesetting?" she could scarcely believe her ears.

"So that's what you're trained for. Journalism," he sneered.

"This is not the dark ages, and I won't be treated like a cave woman. You're not going to drag me around by the hair and control every thing I do or say. Good-bye, Darrin." She slapped the table hard enough to make the lid on the sugar bowl jingle and stormed out the back door. She crawled into her dark green 1989 vintage Chevy pickup truck and backed out of the driveway, clutched, shoved it into low gear, and slung gravel all the way to the back porch of the huge ranch house where Darrin lived with his mother and father.

She was still boiling mad when she crossed the Hendrix Bridge across the Red River separating Oklahoma from Texas. And the fire hadn't gone out one whit by the time she got home to Bells, Texas, just east of Sherman. To think that she'd worked so hard and he expected her to stay at home and not even use her education. It all went to show just how little she really knew the man she was about to promise to love, honor, and . . . obey? He would probably insist on the archaic traditional vows, too. Could she honestly promise in a church full of family and friends, right in the presence of God, Himself, that she would obey Darrin?

She stomped through the house, glad her grandmother wasn't home yet, and threw herself on her bed, expecting the tears to overpower the anger and begin to stream down her face any minute. She was in love with Darrin, so much in love that she'd accepted his proposal. And he'd just let her walk out the door. He'd so much as told her he didn't trust her with another man. But the tears didn't come. And the anger didn't go.

Carson Rhodes shifted his weight in the hammock and gazed up at a squirrel playing in the pecan tree in his backyard. Professor Johnson sure didn't know that he'd torn the lid off Pandora's box today. He'd sat there on the other side of his desk, a king in his old worn-out leather throne, and pronounced sentence upon him and Molly both.

Carson wanted this assignment more than anything he'd ever wanted in his entire life. It was the tip of the iceberg or else his sixth sense was failing him. Professor Johnson's old eyes, set in a bed of wrinkles, twinkled when he told them in class that morning that he'd made his decision about who was going to get the peach assignment. He'd chosen his best two students for the job and asked that Molly Baker and Carson Rhodes meet him in his office right after class.

Carson glanced across the room at Molly to find her staring wide-eyed at him. The diamond on her finger sparkled in the rays of the morning sun filtering through the classroom window. It wasn't a secret that she was engaged or that it almost pained her to even speak to Carson. And now she had to spend two weeks with him in up close and personal quarters. He sure didn't want to be caged up in a truck for two weeks with a very much engaged Molly Baker, and he tried to portray that in the silent message he sent across the room.

"So, are you two going to take this assignment?" the professor asked as he bounced into the room. He plopped down in his chair and turned a pencil this way and that in his hands.

"Yes, sir." Carson nodded but he didn't look at Molly. He might have to fight a legion of demons, but by golly, if she had any she could fight her own. He wasn't about to give up this opportunity just because she had a fiancé.

"Yes, sir," Molly said just above a whisper, knowing full well the fight with Darrin might start the third world war. "But . . ."

"Oh, no, my dear." The professor shook his head, then adjusted his wire-rimmed glasses on his beaklike nose. "There are no buts. Carson is a professional. The best photographer I've ever seen. And your journalism is the most polished I've ever read. He could take a picture of a cow patty and you could describe it, and by the time I got finished reading about it and looking at the picture, my nose would be snarling. I swear I could probably smell it through osmosis. So you two are my choice for this assignment. If you are both willing, I have an expense check for each of you"— he held up two white business envelopes—"plus whichever one of you takes their vehicle can claim mileage and be paid for that when you get home.

There's enough here that if you don't eat steaks and lobster every night you might even make a dime on this venture. But the monetary rewards of this journey aren't the real profit. You'll be tested when you get back, as you well know."

"Why didn't you pick two men or two women?" Molly was visibly bewildered.

"I knew that question was coming." He shook a bony finger at them. "But true journalists, photo or otherwise, in today's world can learn to work together in spite of gender. It's a wonderful time we're living in. Men and women working together, accomplishing great things. I don't see a man and woman sitting before me. I see a team who can put together the best package deal available. Carson can take pictures and you can write. You're on your own with this. It can be as good or as mediocre as you want. The guidelines are here." He handed each of them a folder. "Basically, the company deals in postcards, calendars of all kinds, and his new area we talked about in class. They will be printing a book for a tour of these states. Probably catering to older people, so keep that in mind, Molly. The gray-haired retirees will board the bus in Dallas and come back to that same place ten to twelve days later. And they'll want pictures and writing about each state, each piglet, each ear of corn they pass along the way. So bring me excellent pictures and the best in writing. I'll see you both in two weeks. Got a class now. I'm glad neither of you backed out on me.

I didn't have any alternatives in mind." He was out the door before either of them could ask another question.

Carson picked up his envelope and turned to look at Molly, who slowly reached her hand out to pick hers up from the desk. "I can drive my pickup truck. It's got a shell on the back so we'll have lots of room for our gear," he said.

"Good, because I don't think my old truck would ever make that kind of trip. I've been pampering it just to get to school and back home this past year," she agreed.

"Well, then, shall I pick you up at the dorm? Or do you have an apartment?"

"I live with my grandmother in Bells, Texas," she said, without looking at him. "That's—"

"I know where Bells is. I'm from Sherman," he said. "Just tell me where to go from the corner when you turn . . ."

"Don't go that far. Granny has a little farm a couple of miles back west from there. It's right on the road. White house with yellow trim. Mailbox says Hilda Parker. Can't miss it," she said.

"Then I'll be there at six o'clock Saturday morning." He stood up. "We should make Omaha by suppertime that first day."

She nodded as she put the envelope in her purse, and Carson knew without a doubt that she'd rather be spending two weeks with a rattlesnake in the Sahara Desert than sharing the adventure with him.

The alarm clock startled Molly awake. She slapped it, trying to clear the cobwebs from her mind and remember why she had set such an early alarm on Saturday morning. She sat straight up in bed. This was *the* day. Carson would arrive in only an hour, and they were off for two weeks: all the way to Canada and back. She sighed and reached for the light switch on the wall above her bed.

She would rather the professor had chosen Brad Dalton than Carson, and she could just barely tolerate Brad with his tobacco chewing and swaggering around like he was God's own personal gift to the whole female population. She picked up her hairbrush and tackled her shoulder-length black hair, pulling it up into a ponytail. Black hair from her Cherokee father— her granny's son. Clear blue eyes which defied all genetic rules, since brown eyes are dominant—from her Irish mother.

"You about ready?" Her short, stocky little Indian grandmother peeped inside the room and handed her a cup of steaming black coffee. "Got everything you need in them bags?"

"Yep. I can't believe Darrin hasn't called even one time," she said, straightening the collar on her blue chambray shirt and tucking it into a pair of soft denim jeans. She pulled on her white athletic shoes and tied the laces in neat bows.

"I'm glad he hasn't called, and if you'll just admit it, you are, too. He's not right for you, girl. I been tellin' you that for the past year. He's going to break your spirit and I've worked hard to build that spirit up. You'll shrivel up and die out there on that ranch from daylight to dark. You ain't cut out to be a set-at-home wife," she scolded. Molly listened with half an ear as she put a clean case on her favorite pillow and tossed it on top of her stack of bags.

"Good coffee," she said.

"Strong. Coffee should have some body and flavor. Most people just serve up murdered water." Her grandmother chuckled. "Now that I see you're awake, I'm going back to bed until it's a decent time to get up. Lord knows, I need my beauty sleep. Get on out there and bring back enough stuff to knock that professor's socks off, child. And while you're gone, forget about that worthless Darrin." She stood on tiptoe to kiss Molly on the forehead. "Who knows, you might be off in Alaska this time next year if you do a good job this time."

"Oh, Granny." Molly giggled. "That's too much to even ask for."

Carson found the place with absolutely no trouble. He was only mildly surprised to see Molly swinging in the porch swing when he drove up into the yard. He'd half expected to find her still asleep and then she would moan and groan the whole time she got her things together. She set her cup down on the railing and picked up several bags and a pillow before he could get out of the truck. "Good mornin'," she said cheerfully.

"I'll help you with those," he offered, but she shook her head.

"Just open up the back and I'll toss them in," she said. "What is all that stuff?" She frowned when he lifted the door to the back of the candy apple red truck with a matching shell over the back.

"Gear." He attempted to smile but it came out more of a grimace. This was all he needed—a fussy female who wouldn't appreciate any of his efforts to save a dollar on this trip or to make it an adventure. She'd probably whine and carry on awful at every suggestion. And when he mentioned camping out, she'd go up in six-foot flames and rant and rave about not having a mirror to make sure her mascara was applied properly.

"Oh," she said, and headed toward the passenger door. "Let's get something straight right now," she said when he got back into the truck. "I'm a woman and there's no getting around that fact. But I've got aspirations of being a real journalist some day. One who goes into the far side of Africa to write about a lost tribe of aborigines or to Ireland right in the middle of a revolution. I'm not a pansy, and I don't expect any special treatment."

"Good." Carson nodded. "Because you sure won't be getting any special treatment from me. I want to go to Africa and take the first pictures of that tribe you're talking about, and I want to photograph the devastation of the revolution you mentioned. If I'd had my way I wouldn't be traveling with a woman on this trip. So it's good we've cleared the air."

"Okay, now let's go. We've got a lot to accomplish in the next two weeks. According to this itinerary the tour people gave us, it'll be grueling."

I hope so, he thought as he fired up the engine. *I hope it makes me so tired I forget how blue your eyes are and how beautiful you are. I hope I fall into my sleeping bag so exhausted I forget you are so close I could hear you breathing. That is unless you insist I take you to a motel so you can primp and pamper yourself. I really don't know you at all, but Molly Baker, I sure would like to.*

"So where's the diamond?" he asked as they drove across the Red River Bridge, leaving Texas in their rearview mirror.

"What?" She turned quickly to see him eyeing the indention on her ring finger where the engagement ring had been for the past several months.

"Your ring? Why'd you leave it at home?"

Wrong question, she wanted to shout. *Just take me back home and do your own writing,* she fumed. "That is personal and this is business. Let's don't mix the two," she finally said.

"Just making conversation. Are we going to talk pure business for two weeks, then?" he asked.

She inhaled deeply. "Probably so. Are you going to let that gorgeous sunrise get away from you? There will only be fourteen if the sun shines every day. There's twelve months in a year, so you'll need at least that many for a calendar."

"Yes, ma'am." He pulled off on the side of the road, took his equipment from the backseat of the club cab truck, and set up the tripod to take a picture with a slow shutter speed. The sun was an orange ball through a copse of pecan trees on a slight knoll with a small cemetery in the foreground. A bent, elderly gentleman was laying flowers on a grave and had just stood up when Carson pushed the cable release. The man was just a small silhouette in the foreground, but it gave the picture that unique character he liked in his work. He hoped for at least twelve very different sunrises to make up a whole calendar with a distinct sunrise from each state, just as Molly suggested.

She took out her trusty old ten-cent stick pen and spiralback notebook and began writing about the first picture he took. Someday a little gray-haired lady would look in a tour book and the first thing she'd see would be a beautiful Oklahoma sunrise. It might be that very picture which made the lady book a ticket on the bus. And she would meet a distinguished gentleman traveling on the same tour, and they would fall in love in the twilight years of their life.

She looked up in time to see Carson snap the cover back on the camera lens and shake the legs of his faded jeans back down from where they'd ridden up. The sleeves of his soft white T-shirt stretched tight across his bulging arms, probably the result of hours and hours in a gym, since he didn't have to work to pay for his tuition. He wasn't all that much taller than she was—only five inches, maybe less. She was five feet four inches and he might be five nine, but he would probably have to tiptoe to get that much height. Good-looking beyond words. If he didn't make it taking photographs, he could probably get on the other side of the camera and pose for them.

"Good grief." She laughed to herself. "I'm supposed to be luring people into a tour, not playing matchmaker or sizing up Carson Rhodes, whom I will not like no matter what he looks like or says." She shook her head and went back to writing.

"What's so funny?" He tucked his equipment back into the navy blue bag and crawled back into the truck.

"I was just imagining someone like the professor going on this trip and falling in love with a lady with blue hair and gold lamé sneakers."

"Is that business?" he asked curtly.

"No, it's not," she said, just as icily. So much for even trying to be cordial. He could just sit there and drive, and she would be hanged from the nearest tall pecan tree if she tried to be nice again. He gritted his teeth so hard she could see his jaw working, but she didn't really care. She didn't like men with dark hair, especially dark brown hair and matching brooding brown eyes. After her mother died, when she was just three years old, her Indian father had left her for her grandmother to raise. She had stood on the porch when he left and cried her eyes out, but he didn't even look back. Two years later they got word he'd died in an automobile accident in El Paso. Granny brought his body home and they had a funeral. And Molly made up her mind while she watched the gravediggers fill in the six-foot grave that she would never trust another man with dark hair and dark eyes. Or one that just plain took her breath away with his good looks, either . . . as Carson Rhodes had from the first day he walked into the advanced journalism class. Good-looking men, especially those who knew it, couldn't be trusted as far as she could throw them. She'd proven that when she dated the quarterback of the Whitewright High School football team way back when she was a senior. Not even as handsome as Carson and an ego twice the size of the state of Texas.

So even if he was blond as a Nordic and had eyes the color of grass, she still wouldn't like him. He just exuded too much charm with that big smile of his, complete with a dimple in the right side and a slight cleft in his strong chin. He was just a spoiled-rotten brat who didn't even have to work at a job to get through school. Nope, she'd made up her mind years ago about dark-haired men and pretty boys.

And she wasn't changing it . . . not ever.

Chapter Two

Carson braked suddenly, checked the rearview mirror, threw the truck in reverse, and backed down the highway. He made a right-hand turn at the first dirt section line road and parked the truck. "Buffalo," was all he said to Molly as he picked up his camera from the backseat and traipsed off through the weeds growing between the road and the barbed wire fence.

"Whoopee," she snorted, glad that she had her seatbelt firmly buckled or she would have been thrown through the windshield and ended up on the hood of the truck like the dead bucks the hunters displayed during deer season. She frowned as she undid her seat belt and opened the door. She stuck her pen in the base of her ponytail and grabbed her notebook. She should have brought along the mini-cassette recorder but she just flat forgot it. Besides, her ideas often flowed through the pen like they had a mind of their own. "One big bruiser claiming the whole herd of cows as his special harem. Bet his name is Carson," she said in a barely audible voice.

He was down on one knee holding the camera between the strings of barbed wire. "Postcard material. You just need a couple of lines. There's one similar to it in the folder. Only mine will be better, because I can get the cows in the background and that big old boy is front and center." He inhaled deeply and pushed the button on top of the camera, then turned the camera sideways and took another one. "Give them the choice of vertical or horizontal."

"Only a little bit egotistical," she muttered.

"Does look like that, doesn't he?" Carson smiled.

"Oh my, yes," she agreed, fighting off the urge to giggle. But even if it took biting her tongue off every day and having to grow a new one every night, she was not about to get on friendly terms with Carson or any other man for that matter. Darrin had just proved that marriage was a one-sided paradise for the male gender. Get up in the morning and fix breakfast, cook, clean, and produce children, have a wonderful supper on the table at six sharp, and don't get angry if he doesn't walk through the door until eight.

At mid-morning he stopped to take a picture of a plain old box turtle crossing the road. He waited until the turtle was right on the yellow line before he snapped the picture and she simply wrote "turtle on line" in her notebook beside the number that correlated to his negative number. She'd braced herself just in time to prevent whiplash when he stopped on a whim to take a picture of an antique tractor with wild yellow flowers growing around the tires and a bird's nest complete with eggs in the rusty old seat. She threw her hand out and kept herself from bouncing around when he stopped to take one of coreopsis blooming along a sagging barbed wire fence with a string of blackbirds sitting on it. She'd expected the birds to fly away, but evidently he bewitched them as much as all the girls at the college, because they almost smiled for him when he snapped two pictures . . . one horizontal and one vertical.

As they skirted the edge of Bartlesville he noticed three squatty water towers. One was marked HOT, one WARM, and one COLD. *If I took a picture of Molly she'd have to stand beside the cold one*, he thought. *She'd probably rather be chasing around dress racks over there in that shopping mall as writing about whatever pictures I find.*

A town, she sighed. *Now, just what is he going to find that is so fascinating here. Any minute I expect him to start taking pictures of dead skunks and possums in the middle of the road. Maybe he's got a redneck calendar in mind. You might be a redneck if you think road kill is a form of art.* She didn't even smile at her own ingenuity.

She pulled her pen from her hair and began writing about Bartlesville, Oklahoma, the last town of any size the company in the tour would see as they traveled. Perhaps they'd stop here for mid-morning coffee and a restroom break. She mentioned the humor in three water towers she'd just seen. Hot, warm, and cold. If Carson had his picture taken standing in front of one, it would definitely be the hot one . . . to go with the way all the girls fell at his boot tips just before class time. She'd even overheard one feisty girl say that she'd lay down in the middle of a freeway and die happy if he'd just ask her out to dinner.

Definitely—hot!

When they crossed the line from Oklahoma to Kansas, he pulled off to the side of the road and took a picture of the sign: WELCOME TO KANSAS. Just what was she supposed to write about a welcome sign? Was she going to have to come up with something different for more than a dozen states? ". . . Take a picture of a cow patty and you could write about it." The professor's words came out of the clear blue summer sky to haunt her.

"Get over it," she chastised herself. "You will write about whatever he takes pictures of, as well as the countryside or anything else. This is not a pleasure trip. It's business. Remember we are a team." She sighed.

Sunflowers covering half the blue sign and a few wild sunflowers in the foreground, she wrote in her notebook. Welcome to the land of sunflowers and bright sunny days, where the gentle wind waves the wheat and the people are friendly, she penned as she waited for him to get back to the truck.

"The tour will stop at 'The Little House on the Prairie' thing," she reminded him when she saw the first sign.

"You ever see any of those shows?" he asked.

"Every one of them at least three times," she nodded. "You?"

"Every one of them at least four times," he said seriously.

"You are kidding me." She jerked her head around to look at him. "You really watched that kind of show."

"Sure, and the Waltons too. Still watch them sometimes on early morning television if I don't have a class." He grinned. "Aren't men supposed to watch old reruns?"

"I don't know what men watch except football on Monday nights and blood, guts, and gore movies," she said.

"That what your father watches?" he asked, turning back down a narrow road to the east.

"My father is dead and has been since I was five. I didn't see him from the time I was three, when my mother died with brain cancer," she said. "My granny raised me, so I don't know what men watch. Darrin watches Monday night football and violent movies, and that's what I have to base my opinion on."

"I'm sorry about your parents," he said honestly. "I didn't know. So is Darrin your brother."

"Darrin is . . ." She stopped for a minute. "Darrin is . . ." She stammered, trying to figure out how to tell him that Darrin was her ex-fiancé. Yet, was he really an ex or would they work things out when she got back to Texas? She hadn't cried, and the anger was almost gone. So maybe there was hope.

"Darrin your boyfriend?" he asked.

"I suppose you could put it that way," she said.

"Okay," he sighed, but she didn't catch it. She was too busy looking at the maps and trying to get her heart put back together.

"And yes, I do like the old reruns. Nellie Olson is a spitfire, isn't she? And Mrs. Olson is the first-rate witch of the west. Here we are. Doesn't look like much, but then it will give the folks a chance to stretch their legs a little, won't it?"

"I can just imagine Nellie going to school in here," she said as they stepped into the one-room building. "She'd sit right there with her *boing boing* curls and ribbons in her hair." She turned to find him taking a picture of the school desks. The bottom half of the curtains blew outside the open windows in the background, and she could already visualize the postcard the company would make from the picture. And how many of them would probably sell right here on this small acreage.

They went from the schoolhouse to the post office, which was in the middle of the three buildings. Inside were postcards, books, pens, and other memorabilia from Laura Ingall's famous series, and a lady behind the small desk who was telling a couple with several rambunctious children about the place.

Molly took notes fast and furiously while Carson snapped several pictures at different shutter speeds, with and without a flash. Then they went to the actual cabin, which had been constructed as nearly to the dimensions of the original house as possible.

"Can you imagine really living in something this small?" Carson said as he zeroed in on a photograph of Laura and her husband Almonzo.

"No, but I guess lots of people did," she said.

"Man, they'd have to get along pretty good. There's sure not room in here to have an argument and stomp off to a bedroom down the hall. Scarcely room to cuss a cat without getting a hair in your mouth." He smiled—it was remarkable. They'd exchanged a few cordial words with each other and the day was only half over. They might even be friends by the time two weeks were finished. *Don't expect miracles, boy,* his conscience said bluntly. *It's been plain from day one that she just flat out doesn't like you, even if you don't know why. When the other girls gather 'round to talk, she avoids you like the plague. Don't know why but she's just not drawn to you like you are her. So face it. You might be decent working acquaintances, but there'll be ice skating in Hades before that girl is ever your friend. Besides she is probably still engaged. Even if she couldn't spit the words out about Darrin, evidently she's still in love with him and she did say he was her boyfriend.*

She took notes as he drove. Just cryptic messages to refresh her memory tonight in a motel room. Then she would pull out her laptop computer and really work on writing about the scenery and the towns they went through on Highway 75. He could watch television, sleep, or read, or even go to the exercise rooms in the motel, but she fully well intended to type all night in her room. By the time they got back to Texas she'd have it all written, rewritten, and polished until it gleamed, ready to send away both in hard copy and on a disk.

"There's a campground just outside Omaha I'm staying in tonight. I brought two pup tents in case you're game for adventure. If not I'll drop you at the nearest motel and pick you up in the morning." He burst her little motel bubble before it even was fully formed.

"Campground?" she mumbled. "Tents?"

"There's the Nebraska sign." He stopped the truck and she braced herself again.

NEBRASKA . . . THE GOOD LIFE; she wrote details of the sign on another page in her notebook. HOME OF

ARBOR DAY and picture of what appeared to be a capitol building with a big orange sun behind it. The good life in a pup tent with Carson on the other side of her. Just minutes before she was already thinking about a long hot shower and solitude while she let her creative juices flow. And now all she could think about was playing wilderness woman in a campground.

"Why a campground? I figured we had enough money for motels and food anyway," she asked when they were back on the road.

"I hate motels. I love camping. You don't have to spend the nights in the same spot I do. Nothing in the folder that says that. You can have your soft bed and personal bathroom and I'll pick you up tomorrow morning," he said.

"Are you saying I'm too soft to stay in the great outdoors?" she taunted.

"I'm not saying anything." He slapped the steering wheel. "I really don't care where you stay. I'm here to take pictures and you're here to do the writing. We don't even have to speak if you don't want to. But we've got two whole weeks in this truck together, and it might be a little more pleasant if we're at least cordial. You don't have to slide over here and kiss me goodnight, for pete's sake, Molly. But we are adults and we are interested in the same things, so we could have a little conversation, don't you think? Now if you want to stay in a motel, just tell me and I'll take care of it."

"Well, I'm staying in a tent. How much does this campground stuff cost? We'll split the cost. Does it have an electrical outlet?"

"First one is twenty-two dollars with water and electricity. The highest priced one I've got mapped out is twenty-six or so. I figured if you stayed you'd want electricity for your laptop. Eleven dollars each tonight. Has a picnic table with benches, shade trees, miniature golf if you have time for a round and a game room and pool room. So you won't be out in the utter boonies," he said. "Thought we'd stop in the Old Market for supper and a little sightseeing."

"My, oh my, aren't you the ultimate travel guide," she said. "And what is the Old Market?"

"Never been to Omaha?" he asked.

"Oh, sure. Granny and I just fly up here every few weeks to eat a big steak. Of course, I haven't been to Omaha. I haven't been anywhere except Oklahoma and Texas, and one brief trip to Louisiana. Don't talk down to me, Carson Rhodes. I might not be as well traveled as a rich little boy like you—"

"Wait a minute." He held up his hand. "What makes you think I'm a rich man?"

"New truck. I heard the girls say you even own your own house."

"I spent four years in the Navy, so I get the GI Bill and I get a lot of scholarship money," he said. "I saved every penny I could while I was in the service for this vehicle and for college. I knew I couldn't afford a car payment and go to school both. My folks retired last year. They owned four houses. My father is an only child and he inherited his parent's house down in Corpus Christi when they died. They gave that to my oldest sister since she and her husband live there. My mother inherited her grandmother's home and they gave it to my other sister in Greenville. My house belonged to my mother's brother, who was an old bachelor. They kept the one they raised us children in over in Van Alstyne. I'm certainly not rich, Molly. I have a place to live, a truck to drive, and a check from the GI Bill which plays out this month. If I don't find work after graduation, I'm in big trouble."

"You can always work at a local newspaper taking pictures of football games and writing sports stories." She borrowed Darrin's words with only a slight variation.

"You can have that job," he said.

"Are you saying I can't do the big stuff?" she shot back at him. Evidently, it didn't make a whit of difference if a man was ugly as a mud fence or was a clone of Richard Gere himself. They all thought women and kitchens were synonyms and couldn't do diddly squat.

"Hey, don't get your dander up," he said.

"It is up, and if I don't want to work part-time at a local paper, if I want to go for the adventures . . ." She sucked in a lung full of air.

"Well, I don't want to do that either. I want the

adventures too." He shook his head. "I'll take pictures of welcome to state signs and stuff for calendars the rest of my life before I settle down into a rut. I want to make enough money to live on comfortably, but I'll take my chances. I'd rather take pictures of tourist traps forever as work at a nine-to-five—"

"What you're saying is that you don't want a mediocre life with a secure paycheck every Friday at five o'clock," she said seriously.

"Exactly," he said. "Postcard," he said, and braked again. This time she didn't even come close to bumping her head on the dashboard. She just reached up to get her pen from her ponytail and watched him focus his camera on a black pumping oil well in a field of milo.

San Antonio has the river walk. Galveston the beach. Omaha has the Old Market, a few square blocks in the center of the old part of town where jazz musicians play on the street corners and vendors sell everything from apples to silver jewelry, from ice cream to carved ivory rings. Molly sat down on the curb and wrote as fast as she could put words and notes on paper. She loved it. She wanted to come back again and spend a whole week instead of a few hours. The people on the tour would go absolutely crazy over this little bit of paradise, and she felt an urgency to get it all written. Carriage rides, old-time ice cream store, people milling about everywhere.

"Hungry?" Carson sat down beside her, a saxophone player just behind them playing his heart out while people tossed dollar bills and change into his open instrument case. "Think he gets a paycheck on Friday at five?"

"I'm starving and I want to go down in that thing over there." She pointed toward the doors leading into a passageway between two buildings. "I betcha he's the happiest man in the whole town." She nodded back toward the musician as she closed her notebook. "You're going to have to remember and tell me what you took pictures of. I was so busy writing I didn't even watch you."

"I noticed." He grinned. "But I kept a running tab for you right here." He tore off the top piece of paper from a notepad and handed it to her. "You can probably write something for each one from those notes."

"Thanks, Carson. Now let's go eat. That burger we ate somewhere down in Kansas has just about played out. Do you think they'll have Mexican?"

"You're in Omaha, steak country, and you want Mexican?" He ushered her across the street and into the door of the conglomeration of shops known as The Passageway.

"Sounds good to me, and there's the place," She pointed down the stairs to a line of people waiting to be seated. "You don't see a line like that at the steak place," she said. "So the Mexican must be better."

"You win," he said. "Mexican it is."

"So you've been here before," she asked while they nibbled on picante sauce and chips as they waited for their food.

"Once. When we were just little kids my folks brought us up here then across to Chicago to the museums," he said. "It's a lot more fascinating now than when I was eight years old, though."

He didn't say that he liked the way she looked in the dark basement of an old building with barely enough light to read the menus. He loved the way her black hair glistened in the candlelight, and would have liked to speak right up and tell her that he'd been attracted to her since the first time he saw her in the journalism class. But she was wearing an engagement ring even then, and he didn't trespass on another man's territory. Not then and not now.

She suddenly wondered why she'd found him so despicable. Evidently, first impressions were not always right after all. She'd thought Darrin was the most wonderful, stable man in the world, and look at that mistake. She shivered in spite of the warmth. She'd come within sixty days of marrying that tall, sandy-haired rancher, and only the professor's decision had brought out what Darrin really intended for her to do once they were married. She and Granny were going to shop for a wedding dress after she finished her summer classes. What if she had found out after the honeymoon that he expected her to stay at home and be a full-time wife, giving up all her dreams and hopes?

It was truly a scary question which she was glad she'd never have to answer, because if Darrin came back begging on his knees, she intended to get everything right out in the open. She was going to be a hotshot journalist, and the options were still the same as they were in the kitchen a few days ago. He could accept it or forget it.

"Are you thinking about buying a sax and standing on the street corner." He laced his fingers together in his lap so he wouldn't reach across the table and take her hand in his. She'd pitch a fit hotter than the picante sauce if he touched her—no doubt about it.

"Nope, thinking about what I'm going to write down tonight," she lied glibly, but didn't look at him. "You did say we had electricity and there are some showers somewhere on the premises?"

"Both," he said.

"And tents?"

"Two," he said. "One for you and one for me. Complete with plastic liner on the floor to keep out chiggers and water if it rains. Three zippers—one for a door, the other two to close up the side mesh windows if it does rain. Even have summer-weight sleeping bags. I see you brought your own pillow, so you won't have to use a rock. Got to admit, I only brought one pillow."

"Some provider you are," she said with a sincere,

bright smile that shocked him—but not as much as it did her. Here she was only one day into the journey and already letting her guard down enough to tease and smile at the man.

Chapter Three

There was a table, an electrical pole, and even a small charcoal grill, plus a huge oak tree to shade it all. Molly made a mental note that if they were going to stop every night at a place like this, then they could very well cook supper for themselves also. That would save even more money. She laughed silently at a vision of Carson cooking over a grill. Now wasn't that a hoot. Men didn't cook. They opened cans of soup or sometimes a box of cereal for breakfast. Darrin couldn't even push the button on the toaster, according to his mother. She took her laptop out of the back of the truck and set it on the wooden picnic table, then laid her notebook beside it.

"Okay"—she turned around—"tell me what to do and I'll help get things ready for the night before I get started writing. I'm new at this stuff and don't know a sleeping bag from a Duroc sow I'm afraid, but I'm a quick study."

"I can take care of this while you get your notes typed," he offered.

"Nope, you might not be there when I'm setting up camp when I'm off to the lost tribe in the interior of Africa. Teach me how to do it, Carson." She shook her head.

"Okay, it's really easy. You just put the poles like this and this, and *poof*, the tent is up. They're just one-man tents that fold flat. New technology, you know. We don't have to cut stakes and put up wooden poles. So, watch me one more time. Like this and this, and it's done. Here's your bedroll and your pillow, so crawl inside and make your bed. I'm off to the pool room to see if there's any competition, and then I think I'll swim a couple of laps around the pool."

"All this for only eleven bucks?" she asked.

"Yep, but no air conditioning or private bathrooms. Only the mirror on the pickup truck for your makeup in the morning, and you have to walk over there"— he pointed toward a concrete block building—"for showers and other necessary things."

"Beats bushes and poison ivy for toilet tissue," she said. She heard his laughter as she made her bed and then crawled back out of the tent on her hands and knees. He'd set the tents so close together that if he snored she'd have trouble sleeping, but then if a bear or a big, mean grasshopper tried to get in her boudoir tent, she could scream right out loud and wake him. So it had its disadvantages as well as advantages.

She got busy on her notes and was just about finishes with the first day's travels when he was suddenly at her elbow, his warm breath making her neck prickly. "Where'd you come from?" She brushed an errant strand of hair from her sweaty forehead and wiped her damp hands on her jeans.

"Been standing here for five minutes right behind you," he said.

"You are lying." She shot him her meanest look, the one she reserved for only the harshest punishment. "I could have felt you if you had been there five whole minutes."

"Oh, you got Indian blood, huh? You can smell the rain when it's still five hundred miles away and can see smoke signals at fifty miles." His dimple deepened.

"As a matter of fact, smart aleck, I do have Indian blood. About an eighth Cherokee, to be exact. Granny is half, my father was a quarter, and I'm an eighth," she smarted right back at him.

"So, that's where the long, straight black hair comes from," he said. "But there must be an Englishman in the woodpile somewhere to contribute those blue eyes."

"Irish. My mother was a red-haired Irishwoman with a temper straight from the back side of Hades," she said. "And that's enough about my ancestors. Is it bedtime?"

"Are you good—"

"No, I am not." She blushed.

"I was going to say, 'Are you good at pool?' " He grinned mischievously.

Her cheeks burned even brighter. "I'm the best. I could probably beat you standing on my head and cross-eyed."

"Then we're on," he said. "I'll help you put the equipment back in the truck and we'll lock it down safe, and then we'll just see if you can whip the shark of the Navy."

"Hmmp," she snapped. "We'll just see if the shark of the Navy likes to be defeated. What's the stakes?"

"Loser has to get up thirty minutes early and get breakfast ready," he said.

"You're on, cowboy." She smiled again, and his heart threw in a couple of extra beats. "Bet you cook some real mean Cheerios, huh?"

He was awake before his alarm went off the next morning. He stretched all the kinks from his back before he unzipped his tent and found the cooking supplies in the back of the truck. A skillet, blue granite coffee pot, couple of matching plates and cups, and silverware for two. He shook a layer of charcoal from the paper bag he'd brought from home and lit it and waited until the coals were white around the edges.

Then he filled the coffee pot with water and measured out just the right amount of grounds to make a full-bodied coffee. While that was brewing, he brought out a cooler from the back of the truck and opened his portable ice box. Bacon, eggs, and bread for toast.

Molly awoke to the sizzling sound of bacon frying and the aroma of fresh coffee. Bless Granny's heart. She'd gotten up early and was fixing breakfast. Then she remembered where she was and what she was doing there. She threw back the edge of the sleeping bag and unzipped her tent door and crawled out to face the morning. The sun was a sliver of orange on the horizon, not even a half-ball yet, and the trees were still just black blobs with a few beckoning limbs reaching out to her. She stretched, her cotton nightshirt inching up her thighs, causing Carson to inhale deeply. Uncle Joe used to say that women like Molly were built like a two-hole outhouse, and not a brick out of place. Her waist was small, and her hips rounded and matched to the top half perfectly. If she cut off all that beautiful hair she'd look a lot like the cartoon character Betty Boop, except her face wasn't as round or her mouth quite as full.

"Well, loser, I see you've got breakfast going? Where did you find all those goodies? I expected Cheerios or a real gourmet breakfast. That's Cheerios with a banana cut up on top." She peeked over his shoulder at the bacon draining on paper towels and watched him crack the eggs and slide them expertly into the skillet.

"Hey, you won, fair and square," he said. "And I'm not a sore loser. How do you like your eggs?"

"Cooked and lots of them," she said. "I'll start with four."

"You're not bashful." He flipped the eggs over, let them cook a minute, and dished them up on a plate. He added a handful of bacon and gave the plate to her.

"Toast?" She raised a dark eyebrow.

"As soon as my four eggs are done," he said. "Then I'll pour out the grease and toast the bread in the skillet."

"Sounds good to me. I'll pour the coffee." She picked up a hot pad from the table and wrapped it around the handle of the pot.

"Mmm." She made appreciative noises as she ate breakfast. "You're going to miss that sunrise and there's a hawk sitting in the top of the tree. Hurry up, Carson, he'll fly away," she said excitedly.

He eased over toward the truck and took two pictures. One of the hawk in front of a big orange sun and the other just as he flew with wings spread wide open. It was a fluke he'd caught such a sight on film, and he grinned from one ear to the other when he got back to the breakfast table.

"Pretty impressive, huh?" he said.

"Yes, it was," she nodded. "That picture may be on the cover of *National Geographic*."

"Oh, sure." His pride puffed up almost as big as his heart.

"I'm serious. It was a good shot." She drank the last of her coffee. "And you make good coffee, too. It's not murdered water. That's what Granny calls weak coffee. It is now fifteen minutes until seven, and the wagon train leaves soon. So we'd better wash dishes and get on down the road and see if you can do any better than that hawk picture today."

"Yes, ma'am," he said.

Corn. Everywhere there was corn. She'd thought that when they crossed the Nebraska state line that things would change, but they didn't. There was another sign, IOWA, YOU MAKE ME SMILE; and not too far over into the state there was a metal sculpture of corn with the front half of a pig on one side and the front half of a cow on the other. So apparently, folks in Iowa grew corn, cows, and hogs. Carson stopped—on a dime again—and took two pictures of the sculpture. Even as she jotted down a brief description of the gentle rolling hills behind the sculpture, most of them covered with none other than corn, she thought about what Carson had said that morning when she awoke and found him actually cooking breakfast.

I'm not a sore loser, he'd said. It was too bad Darrin couldn't have that attitude. He could have called her before she left and at least said he was sorry.

"I've never seen so much corn in my whole life,"

she said when they were back on the highway. "There can't be that many cornbread-eating people in the whole world."

"Oh, but it can be used for something else," he said. "Remember that creek back in Nebraska yesterday. Whiskey Run Creek?"

"Forgot about that," she said, as she made notes about the terraced planting on the rolling hills, the tassels of the corn swaying in the gentle breeze like waves on the sea. "Hey, look over there." She motioned to the side of the road.

As usual, he stopped abruptly, but this time she didn't even notice. The sign was hand-painted in big letters and said FRESH CORN 3 BUCKS A DOZEN. "Are you going to take a picture of that?" she asked, bewildered. What on earth was she going to write about a sign? But she could describe a cow patty, she reminded herself.

"Nope, I'm going to purchase supper," he said. "A dozen should do us a couple of nights, right?"

"You bet," she nodded, already planning to stop by a market and buy a couple of big thick pork chops to go with the corn.

By noon they were at the far edge of the state and stopped at a welcome center called the Top of Iowa. It was a red barn-shaped building complete with a silo and all kinds of brochures and information inside, including a bake sale in the upstairs section. Carson paid for the corn so she bought two loaves of fresh, home-made bread for their supper.

In the gift shop she found corn-shaped suckers and purchased two, stuffing them in her purse for later when they needed something to nibble on. She studied the brochures as he drove and tried to glean a little extra information from each state.

"A well-trained child," she said aloud.

"Me?" he asked.

"Iowa"—she wrote as she talked—"Iowa is a well-trained child who sits quietly and patiently at the dinner table. It minds its manners and says 'please' and 'thank you'."

"Philosophical," he said.

"There is no wildness in Iowa. Even the trees appear to be planted in the perfect spots, and the wilderness has been conquered. It's peaceful and pleasant and"—she changed from the monotone to a wild, crazy voice—"the corn will rise up and devour you at night while you sleep in your pup tent. It will drag you into the middle of the fields and turn you into a candy sucker, and then the robots who really look like people will sell you to unsuspecting tourists." She yanked the two suckers from her purse and handed him one.

He chuckled, then laughed, then roared. So she had a sense of humor to go with those great legs. He took the sucker from her hands, unwrapped it, and stuck it in his mouth. "Wonderful. This tastes like a Texan for sure. Southern and sweet."

"Oh, no," she wailed. "I've got an old Yankee. It's sour and tough. And there is the welcoming doo-hicky for Minnesota, so you better stop."

"But we just stopped not twenty minutes ago," he argued.

"And twenty minutes ago I didn't need to find the ladies room, but I do now, so take this exit, right now, Carson." She pointed hurriedly at the ramp, and he swung into the right lane of traffic just in time.

She made a fast trip through the restroom and re-combed her hair, putting it back up in a ponytail while she had access to a mirror bigger than the palm of her hand. She found Carson, camera slung over his shoulder by a wide strap, grinning as she jogged over to his side.

"Come around back of this place. I've got something beautiful to show you. It's the twin sister of that child you were talking about in the truck."

"Who?" she cocked her head off to one side.

"You know. Iowa is the well-trained child at the dinner table. Well, I just found that child's other half. The bad twin. The untamed one." He almost reached out and grabbed her hand to pull her along but stopped himself short.

"Look." He led the way down a flight of steps and pointed to a wooden arched bridge to the other side of a walking trail.

"It's beautiful," she said. "And not a stalk of corn anywhere in it." They walked across the bridge and

Carson stopped to take at least a dozen pictures along the way. She looked down from the side expecting to see a bubbling stream but there was no water, just a bridge connecting one part of the park to the other. A sudden sadness filled her heart. Darrin hadn't been willing for a bridge. She could have easily been his wife on one side of the park and just strolled across the bridge and been a crack pot journalist on the other side.

"Stand right there and look back at me," he said.

"Hey, I'm not supposed to be in the travel log book," she told him.

"This is with a different camera. One I brought along for my own personal pictures," he explained. "I'll get double copies made and you can have some." He zeroed in on her while she stood in the middle of the bridge and glanced back at him. "So, is this the untrained child?"

"The bridge and all the work make it an educated child but not a conformed one. Kind of like me and you, Carson," she said, with just a hint of sadness.

"Oh, are we educated and not conformed, then?" He grinned as he crossed to where she stood in three easy strides.

"Yes, we are," she said. "Educated to do a job we both love and enjoy, and yet not willing to settle down and do a routine job. We want the wilds and the untouched world at our fingertips."

"You got that right." They crossed the bridge together and followed the trail through the masses of trees back to his vehicle. "Oh, there's my sign," he said. "WELCOME TO . . ."

"MINNESOTA," she droned. "A stone sign with big red letters in the shape of the state. What shall I write about Minnesota?"

"Who knows, but I bet you think of something." He shot two frames, the typical one horizontal and one vertical. "This is where the route changes. We get off on a state highway and take the blue-haired ladies and distinguished gentlemen through some kind of national forest."

She pulled her seatbelt across her chest, picked up her notebook, and slid her pen from her hair. Without a word, she began describing the little trail and the bridge while the picture was still engraved in her mind. She wrote words but questions bombarded her mind. Why couldn't Darrin see the beauty through her eyes just once? Why couldn't he be a little more like Carson?

Now just exactly where did that thought come from? She frowned at herself as she scribbled notes. *Carson might not be the ogre I thought he was in the beginning, but I'm not willing to admit I was totally wrong about him. Put him back in the halls at the college and I'll just bet he'd be in his glory with all the women flocking around him like bees around a honey pot.*

"Got it all down?" he asked.

"Every bit of it," she answered.

Chapter Four

Molly grilled the pork chops while Carson shucked six ears of corn, slathered them with soft margarine, wrapped them in aluminum foil and laid them on the back end of the grill. He used the coffee pot to boil water for iced tea and set their blue granite plates on the picnic table with the silverware placed neatly on a paper napkin beside them.

"Fifty cents more for this place than the last one, and we don't even have golf or a pool or even a game room. How am I supposed to beat you in pool so I don't have to cook breakfast?" she fussed.

"That's why I chose this camp," he teased. "Now you'll have to rise and shine at the same time I do, and we'll share the duties, just like now." He didn't add that he was enjoying these tasks way too much for a man on a business trip with a woman who was probably still engaged to someone else.

"Hmmp," she snorted. "Open the bread and cut the cheese. I'd heard Wisconsin had good cheese, but that stuff just makes my mouth water thinking about it," she said. "Smart people back there at the cheese store, giving out samples like that. What exactly do you plan to do the rest of the evening while I organize my notes and get my writing done. Oh, Wisconsin, land of farms and trees, white egrets, and a few marshes. Not the well-behaved child that Iowa is. Not the errant child which Texas always is, but somewhere in between, with the best cheese in the whole world."

"Maybe they'll send us to Holland next, and you can taste a different kind of cheese." He fed her a bite of white cheese. When his fingers touched her mouth a shock ran through both of them. Instant high color reddened her cheeks, and he jerked his hand away like he'd been burned. Strange, Darrin never produced that sensation even when he kissed her. But then Darrin had never fed her a chunk of Wisconsin cheese before. Matter of fact, Darrin had never fed her anything before. It would have been beneath his macho image to ever do something so romantic. Romantic! Now that's all she needed—to start thinking like that. She quickly turned around to the grill and flipped the pork chops over again.

Whoa, boy, he told himself as he shoved his hand

in his pocket. *This ain't the time or place for things for that. So just settle down.*

"So what are you going to do all evening?" she broke the uncomfortable silence.

"I'm going to stretch out flat in my tent on top of my sleeping bag and read. I brought *N is for Noose* by Sue Grafton and *The Client* by John Grisham, plus a Harry Kemelman and a dozen John D. McDonald paperbacks. And if I get in a really classical mood, I brought *Tom Sawyer* to read again for the nine hundredth time."

"Oh, if I get done before the light is gone, can I borrow a John D. McDonald? I don't care which one it is, long as it's got Travis McGee in it. I might even read by lamplight if I don't get done in time. I didn't think to bring a single book. Didn't realize there would be time for anything but grueling work," she rattled on without caring.

"Did you cry when you found out John D. had died?" Carson asked.

"Wept like a baby," she nodded. "Me and Granny almost had a private wake for him. We pouted around for a week, then started rereading everything he'd written."

"Me, too. I didn't actually cry but I sure did go into a blue funk mood." He was glad for some common ground to escape that feeling when he touched her lips with his fingertips.

"Let's eat and I'll get to my business, then." She

laid a pork chop on each plate and picked up the ears of corn with a hot pad. "Pretty good supper for a couple of journalists on their first lark." She picked up her napkin.

"First, but maybe not the last," he said, his voice barely above a whisper.

"Maybe not." She bit into the ear of corn and rolled her eyes. "I haven't eaten corn this good since I was a little girl and Granny took me to the Chickasaw Festival up in Tishomingo, Oklahoma. That's where she's from." She wiped butter from her chin.

"Oh, and what kind of festival is that?"

"A big one. Whole town participates, since it's the capital of the nation. They served pashofa and corn that tasted almost this good," she said between bites. "Wonder if they grow corn in the village of our lost African tribe?"

He caught the word *our* even though she didn't realize what she'd said. He smiled. "I imagine they grow some fine corn in that village, and maybe they even make good pashofa . . . whatever the devil that is."

She giggled and the sound was music to his ears. "It's a bean dish. Maybe some big magazine will let us cover the Chickasaw Festival some year, and I'll feed you pashofa."

"I'm looking forward to it," he told her. *Only don't feed it to me with your hands,* he thought silently, sneaking peeks at her while he ate. *I'm not so sure I could stand it.*

                            *   *   *

She stretched out in her tent, both of the zippered windows open to let the natural light through. She was grateful for the fine mesh, which kept the gnats and mosquitoes out, but even more so when she thought about grasshoppers which she hated with a passion. She fluffed her pillow, stuffed it under her chest so she could prop up to read, and opened the first page of *The Green Ripper*. She began to read the book for at least the third time. Later, when the other campers had finally gone to bed and the showers were empty, when the hot sun finally set over behind the trees and it was a little bit cooler, she would go take a long cool shower.

The whole two days had been more relaxing than she would have ever imagined. She loved the creative end of the job. Getting the work ready for the tourists. But even the one-line quips for Carson's postcards and the two or three words for the calendar ideas were fun. He'd started a new and different idea that day—taking photos of unusual shots in old cemeteries. The idea sparked after that first day's sunrise with the old gentleman in the foreground. He'd mentioned it to her, and she told him about Granny's friend who visited old cemeteries wherever she traveled and brought back stories about them. There might be other people who appreciated those kind of pictures and wouldn't think they were morbid. One of the last things she'd written before she finished for the day was a line about the entrance to an ancient family cemetery they'd passed. The entry was a wandering red rose crawling up an arbor. She wondered what kind of stories the family members put to rest in that place could tell. Were they pioneers from the East Coast? Did they settle in Wisconsin because they found good fertile ground to plant their corn?

She sighed and realized she was on page four and didn't remember a single word she'd read. She shook the cobwebs from her head and turned back to the first page. She glanced over at the tent beside hers. Carson was lying flat on his back with his book up in the air above his head. No wonder he had such muscled arms. If she held a book like that for very long, her arms would be aching. He didn't know she was staring, so she just drank her fill of him for once. He really was handsome—but there was some substance there, too. He wasn't like the good-looking football player who broke her heart when she was just a teenager. Maybe she'd been too rough on dark-haired men all these years. But that didn't matter anyway. Molly Baker wasn't stupid or egotistical. She was honest when she looked in the mirror. And the woman looking back at her would never catch Carson Rhodes' eye, let alone his heart.

Carson felt her looking at him but he kept his eyes on the John Grisham book. He didn't need to stare at her to know what she looked like. The pages of the book became a miniature screen for Molly's actions these past couple of days. There she was swinging in the porch swing, already dressed and ready to go, which was one point in her favor. And there she was on the bridge, eating a corn shaped candy sucker, pushing her hair back with the back of her hand as she wrote in her notebook; bossing him around telling him to take a picture when she saw it first; and in front of the six-foot mouse replica at the entrance to the cheese store she liked so well.

The waitress brought them a menu and a glass of water each. They both made a face when they sipped the water and smiled at each other. They didn't need words to tell each other that it was the most horrible tasting water they'd had since they'd left home.

"So, you ready to order or do you need a few minutes?" she asked.

"I'm ready," Molly said. "I want Hawaiian chicken, white rice, egg rolls, and hot and spicy soup. And sweet tea to drink."

"Make that two, except I want fried rice." Carson handed back the menus.

"Where you from? I haven't heard talk that southern since a party of military men came in here more than a month ago. I think they said they were from Georgia," the waitress said.

"We're from Texas," Molly said cheerfully.

"On your honeymoon?" she asked.

"Oh, no!" Molly blushed scarlet.

"Well what else would bring you up here all the way from Texas?" she asked.

"Business trip," Carson said. "We're doing a photojournalism trip for a tour guide company with its base in Dallas."

"I see." The waitress winked at Molly and disappeared.

"Excuse me," Carson slipped out of the booth and went off in the direction of the men's restroom. The waitress set a bowl of steaming hot, spicy soup in front of Molly. She put two tall, frosty glasses of iced tea beside their dinner napkins and shook her head in disbelief.

"You sure you aren't pulling my leg?" she asked.

"I'm sorry?" Molly didn't think she'd heard her right.

"You really are up here on your honeymoon, aren't you? The way that fellow looks at you practically made my heart sing a love song. If a man looked at me like that I'd have him to the courthouse so fast it would make him dizzy," she said. "This isn't really a business trip, not that it's any of my business, but I can usually spot honeymooners a mile away. Come through here on their way to Niagara Falls sometimes. Never knew what they saw in that tourist trap when Chicago has twice as much to offer. Go to the museums. Lay out on the beach at the lakeside. Lots of good food. Theaters. You name it, we got it, including some of the best hotels in the world."

"We really aren't married," Molly assured her.

"Well, don't give up hope, girl. That man is in love with you or my hair isn't gray," the waitress whispered when she saw Carson returning to the table.

"Mmm," he muttered, "this sure smells good. It's been months since I ate Asian food."

"It is good. Hot enough to make your nose run. We may be so full we don't even want to eat supper tonight. Which reminds me, where are we staying? Will we make it to Canada?"

"Could, but I thought we'd stop early at a campground on this side of the river. That would make us get to Niagara Falls tomorrow afternoon, and we could spend the rest of the day playing there and then cross the river back into New York to spend the night." He dipped into the soup again.

"Sounds like a good plan to me." She downed a third of the glass of tea, but it didn't quench the fire in her throat or the heat in her heart put there by what the waitress said. She'd have to sort that all out later. Surely, the waitress had just been reading too many romance novels, but it was strange that she'd say something like that to a complete stranger. They'd found, for the most part, the further north they traveled, the less people talked to strangers.

"The lake was absolutely beautiful. I'm glad we

drove down the highway right beside it." She ate the fiery soup a little slower.

"That's the way the tourists will go. The bus will stop and let them eat lunch somewhere. Think we could recommend this place?" he asked.

"Oh, yes. Got a friendly waitress, which is pretty uncommon up here." She smiled. "Guess I better write up a pretty, flowing description of the lake, huh? One like . . . the magnificent rocks tumble into the water like pebbles from a child's sand bucket. The sky and water are the same color of azure, meeting on the horizon in a beautiful blending."

"That's almost mushy," he laughed. "Sounds like a brochure for honeymooners. Maybe the waitress put ideas into your head."

"I don't think so," she sing-songed. "I'm not getting married until I'm fifty years old, and by then I should know better."

"Oh, really." He raised an eyebrow in a gesture she was beginning to find both frustrating and fascinating.

"Oh, really," she shot right back.

"Then is the engagement with the rich rancher off?"

"That, Carson Rhodes"—she accented every word with a shake of her spoon in his face—"is absolutely none of your business. So we'll talk about something else. Would you ever want to live in a place like this? Mercy, but it's too big for this Texan. I look at all those huge factories and buildings and my heart yearns for plain old Sherman, Texas."

"Why is it none of my business?" His voice carried an edge.

"Because I said it isn't. Now answer my question about living here," she said, just about the time the waitress brought their egg rolls and entree.

"Refill that tea for you?" she asked.

"Yes, ma'am." Carson handed his glass to her.

"Whew, I like a man that says ma'am." She whistled through her teeth. "If I was thirty years younger I might even wink at you."

"And if I was ten years older I might wink back," he flirted blatantly.

The waitress laughed heartily and patted his shoulder. "Texas men. If you're all this charming, you can visit my restaurant any day of the week." She went to another corner to wait on another table.

"Where were we?" he asked.

"We were discussing if we could live in Chicago?" she told him.

"Together?" he teased.

She blushed. "Carson!"

They stopped that night at a camp spot in Port Huron, Michigan, arriving at four o'clock in the afternoon. Carson stopped in the middle of the afternoon to take pictures of a drive-in theater still in business and sporting a marquee listing three of the most current movies. He asked her if she'd ever been to a drive-in picture show.

"No," she answered.

"Me, neither. If it was dark and we were ready to call it a day we'd go, just to see what it would be like," he said.

And I'm glad it's not, she thought. *If I remember right most of the time the folks in the vehicle didn't watch the movie so much as they . . .* She blushed again, just thinking about Carson kissing her.

Good grief, she fussed at herself while she took notes about the countryside and a set of photos he took of a neatly kept little cemetery with a huge old oak tree in the middle of the tombstones. *I'm twenty-three years old. I've been kissed and had more boyfriends than I can count on my hands and toes. So why does he affect me like this? I'm a grown woman and Professor Johnson sent us out here to do teamwork. Without gender, I think he said.*

They unpacked the tents and set up camp for the third night. She could scarcely believe it was just three days since she'd left Texas. It seemed like it was a lifetime ago. When they'd gone through a little town called Decatur this afternoon she had a sudden surge of homesickness. Not Darrin-sickness, which surprised her. Somewhere deep down inside her heart she figured there was still a string of love firmly attached to his heart. Surely she'd loved him with her whole being to accept his proposal and begin planning a wedding for September.

But when she thought of Decatur, Texas, all the way

up there in Decatur, Michigan, it wasn't with any heartache for Darrin and what might have been. She hadn't shed a single tear those two days she waited for him to call, and there wasn't a delayed reaction while she grilled chicken breasts for supper that night either. If she was truthful with herself, there was only a sigh of relief that she had escaped a bad choice. What she really missed was her grandmother and best friend, Brenda, who was pregnant with her second child already. Twenty-three, married five years, a lovely little blond-haired girl, and now pregnant again. And Brenda and her husband Tom were at the beach in Galveston, so she didn't even know about the fiasco with Darrin.

"So what's your claim to fame with chicken?" Carson broke her sentimental train of thought. "Last night it was Worcestershire and brown sugar on the pork chops. What are you up to this time?"

"I cut the breast in half longways but not all the way. Made a pocket, kind of. Then I put a fresh jalapeño pepper in the middle and wrapped some of your breakfast bacon around the outside, as you can see." She pointed with her long-handled fork. "We'll cook them slow, eat some more of that delicious corn, although it seems a shame to pay for it when we could harvest a dozen ears right next to the highway and save three dollars."

"Molly Baker!" Carson chuckled. "You'd steal from the good farmers of Michigan!"

"Honey, they've got enough corn in this part of the world to feed every hungry child in the world. They wouldn't miss a few ears," she said. "We got any cheese left? Oh, and I bought some strawberries for dessert. We'll take the ends off and pour fresh whipping cream over them."

Honey, he smiled. It had come out pretty natural and she hadn't even known she'd said it, but she had and it was music to his ears. "You're going to make me fat as the Pillsbury Doughboy."

"I doubt it. And while we're talking food and not job. I'll do breakfast tomorrow morning if you'll do supper. I shopped for it while I was getting the chicken and strawberries. That way I can work on my writing sooner," she said.

"Deal." He reached out his hand to shake with her, only mildly surprised that the same old jolt was there when their hands touched as when his fingertips touched her lips.

It was going to be a long two weeks.

Chapter Five

Molly leaned on the concrete pillar, her chin in her hands as she desperately tried to put the emotions filling her heart into some kind of organized wording. Two magnificent falls. But the feeling in her heart, the breathlessness, the omnipotence of something with so much splendor, could never be put into just mere words. She'd just have to describe it as best she could and let the tourists stand in the mist and be engulfed in the same emotion gripping her at that moment.

Carson was shooting from every angle imaginable as he took pictures of one falls, then the other, climbing steps to the balcony of a restaurant and gift shop for an even better shot. People were everywhere, in great throngs, marching from one end of the walkway to the other; laughing, talking, soothing tired and hot

children. But Molly was so engrossed in simply standing in the mist floating upward from the sheer force
of the water coming over the rocks that she didn't even
see them. The mist reminded her of a fine Texas driz-
zling rain as it soaked her T-shirt and shorts. Her black
hair hung in limp strands, and tears stung her eyes.

"Hey, you're all wet." Carson laughed at her elbow.

She nodded, afraid to trust her voice.

"Looked long enough? Ready to go check out the
tourists traps?"

She shook her head and braced her chin back on
her hands, shut her eyes, and tried to burn the sight
into her mind forever. She might go to Africa someday
or to Alaska as Granny so jokingly suggested, but this
day would always be a milestone. They'd reached the
tip of their journey, and although there might be gorgeous sights on the way back through the rest of the
states, this would be the highlight for Molly. Something about the falls put her own thoughts and prob-
lems in perspective and brought peace to her soul.

Carson put the cap back on the lens and followed
her lead, leaning on the same concrete pillar, his elbow
just inches from hers, and let the magnitude of the falls
overcome him. It wasn't just a picture or description
for a traveler's guide. It wasn't just water falling over
the rocks in a great spill, or even the people in the
Maid of the Mist boats as they traveled under the falls
in their yellow slickers. It was something more, something Molly felt. Suddenly he understood as his heart

melded with hers, and they were more than just journalists on a job.

It was as if they truly captured the spirit at the same time. Their minds worked in unison without a single word. The reason so many people came to Niagara Falls for their honeymoon wasn't because of the tourist traps. It wasn't to buy T-shirts, eat hot dogs on sticks, and stay in motels, whether of the 1950s vintage or the brand-new ones, complete with Jacuzzis. It was to stand together as he and Molly were standing right then and look at something so much bigger than what they were.

Professor Johnson surely put a lot of faith in her, she thought, as she found a smile hidden deep. Because describing a cow patty and making his nose snarl would be nothing to describing this and making tears fall out over the tops of his twinkly old eyes. Maybe this was the test he was talking about. The one whether he'd know for sure if she passed the class.

"I'm ready now," she said when she could trust her voice to come out past the lump the size of a baseball in her throat. "Do we really get to play all afternoon? And not have to write a single sentence about what we saw while we did it?"

"Yes, we do," Carson said. "But I cannot imagine not taking a picture of anything or you not making your fingers fly over the keyboard tonight telling what you did. It's kind of in our blood, isn't it, Molly?"

"Granny says success is loving your job so much

it's part of you." She turned her back on the falls but swung around quickly for one last peek, just in case she'd forgotten some tiny aspect.

"Then I think we're probably the most successful people in the whole world." He longed to put his arm around her and tell her he shared her deepest emotions and feelings, but he hesitated and the moment passed.

They'd paid five dollars to park the truck in a lot and it was good until midnight, so they opted to walk and do their sightseeing. Carson was only faintly amazed that she didn't whine or gripe about exercise. He thought she might be a poor sport the day he arrived at her house and found her on the porch swing. But she'd sure proved her mettle. This morning he awoke to the smell of sausage frying and another aroma which turned out to be Indian fry bread, a soft skillet-fried biscuit that went wonderfully well with sausage and scrambled eggs. She'd crawled inside her tent at night like a true trooper and out in the morning with a smile on her face, ready to go again. She typed relentlessly in the evenings but still had time for a quick swim if there was a pool and didn't even whine if she had to swim in a creek. So far he couldn't fault her one time. She was just as good a traveling companion as any fellow would have been.

"This walking is wonderful," she said after a long, comfortable silence. "I was beginning to think my whole body was going to be in the shape of a pickup seat. I've never sat still so long in my whole life."

"Might be doing a lot of that, if you make it big in the world of journalism," he said. "Lots of flying. Lots of sitting still waiting for something to happen. Lots of typing at night into the wee hours of the morning so you can get it on paper before you forget."

"Maybe so, but there will be days like this when I have to walk forever to make up for it. There's an ice cream parlor. Let's go in and sit in those little bistro chairs and stuff our faces." She headed in that direction before he could answer.

"I want a strawberry sundae with lots of whipped cream and nuts," she told the lady at the counter.

"Make mine the same except chocolate," he said right behind her.

"Where you two from?" she asked. "Not Alabama or Georgia?"

"Texas," Molly looked at Carson and laughed—sincere, open and mischievously.

"I knew it was somewhere down there. What are you doing up here all the way from Texas?" she asked. "Honeymooning?"

"How'd you guess?" Carson picked up the lighthearted spirit.

"Oh, I can tell when two people are in love." She giggled.

Molly chuckled as she dove into her sundae. "So we're honeymooners, are we? Well then, husband, after we eat all these grams of fat, shall we go do whatever it is newlyweds do in Niagara?"

"Kiss?" he raised both eyebrows, wrinkling his forehead and bugging out his big brown eyes. "Really?"

She slapped him on the upper arm, only slightly surprised at the sensation when her palm touched his skin. "No! We're just going to play-act, and then when I write up my story, the little blue-haired lady and the distinguished gentleman with wire-rimmed glasses will know that when they get to this place they can pretend they're honeymooners. Who knows, by the time they get home they might even be ready to book another trip for their real honeymoon," she said.

"Never know," he said. "Okay, wife, what would you like to do next? Go ride the elevator all the way to the top of the sky to see the whole area? To look from this country over into the United States?"

"Sounds good to me. I won't get sick, will I?"

"Let's hope not." He laughed.

Clouds scuttled over the sun as it tried to go down in a blaze of glory over a perfect day when they checked into their campground near Buffalo, New York, that night. Carson took several pictures of the unusual sunset in an array of pinks, purples, and bright white lines around the dark clouds, then set up the tents while she got out her computer and began to work.

"Thought we'd have supper at the snack bar," he offered. "We've eaten junk food all day and . . ."

"I want a hamburger and french fries and a big Diet

Coke." She didn't look at him but slipped a disk into the slot and started typing, words flowing from her fingertips to the screen like water through a sieve. "And thanks, Carson, for a lovely day and suggesting we not cook tonight. I'm hungry for a good old greasy burger someone else cooks after all that junk, and I do want to get this all down. You going to play some mini-golf while I work?"

"No, I think I'll stretch out and read. Had all the walking I want for one day," he said. "Mustard on your burger?"

"How'd you know?" She looked up into his soft eyes and for just a split second saw something there she hadn't noticed before.

"Mustard, double the pickles and onions, no tomatoes and light on the lettuce," he said. "Same way I like mine."

"Right on." She laughed like she did in the ice cream parlor.

"Be right back," he said.

She typed until after dark. When she finished and read back over her report she was amazed that she'd actually found the right way to describe the whole day. Not too flowery. Not nearly as emotional as she'd really felt standing there in the presence of something so powerful. Just good descriptive phrases which should draw tourists to the falls. And then they could shed their own little tear as the mist fall around them like a cloak.

He stretched out in his tent and attempted to read, but the events of the day kept coming back to haunt him. Molly's giggle in the ice cream parlor when the girl told them they were honeymooners. As magnificent as this place was, as heart-rending as it was to stand there in the mist with Molly, as much fun as they'd had today roaming around with no place they had to be and nothing they had to do, he wasn't so sure if he'd ever bring a bride to this place. Too many people. When he married he fully well intended that he and his new bride would be on a remote island for a couple of weeks.

"Done." She clicked the Save button and waited while the computer churned out the information. Then she pulled out the disk and labeled it with the subject and date, then put it in a padded, waterproof heat-resistant case. "Carson, are you at a stopping place?" she raised her voice just slightly.

"Yes." He didn't tell her that he'd been watching her expressions for the past hour. Some Indian she was. She didn't even know he'd watched her relive the whole day as she put it on paper. Or that he'd seen her wipe the steady stream of tears from her cheeks at one time, probably when she saw the enormity of the falls on the screen of her computer, only this time in words and not reality.

"Then let's go watch one of those free movies this

place offers. We paid high dollar, all of thirteen fifty each to stay here. We might as well get a little of the benefits before we leave." She put her computer back in its carrying case.

"Okay," he said. "What do you want to see? They've got a whole bunch of movies and a couple of rooms with television sets and VCR's. Here, you better let me put that back in the truck before we leave. Best not take a chance and leave it out."

"You want blood, guts and gore?" She noticed he needed to shave. Strange, she didn't remember him having such a dark beard before, but then it was getting late in the day.

"Not necessarily," he took his T-shirt off and put it in a laundry bag and pulled a clean one over his head. Just when did he get so muscular? She gasped.

"Then if they have it, could we watch *Something to Talk About* with Julia Roberts? I missed it when it came out way back when," she said.

"If they have it, that's fine with me," he said.

It was available and no one else was interested in the old movie. As a matter of fact, no one was interested in movies at all that evening. Probably all the campers came with television sets and VCRs, and they were lying around in comfortable pajamas watching Mel Gibson tear up the bad guys in *Lethal Weapon IV*. All six copies of that movie were checked out already. The room was set up with six recliners in a semicircle. She leaned back in one, and he sat down beside her and did the same. They laughed until their faces hurt, but when she cried at the sad places, she just wiped the tears away and didn't look at Carson. Were all men like that? Cheating? Demanding? And did all marriages end up in a rut? Or did they go through tough times and in the end get back on track like the couple did in the movie? Would she go home and find Darrin standing at her doorstep with a dozen roses, her ring in his hand and an apology on his lips?

And if he is, I may call Julia's aunty from the movie and see what it was she gave her to pour in that food to make him sick, she thought with a grin. *Sometimes it's too late to say I'm sorry and it's too late to do what you should have done in the first place. And I'm beginning to think anything we could have shared died that day when he said I couldn't go and stay engaged to him. But when someone dies there is a mourning period, and even yet she had not grieved for the marriage she was supposed to have.*

"So, you ready to get married now?" he asked as they walked back to the campsite. The moonless sky was covered with dark clouds, and not a single twinkling star could be seen anywhere.

"When I'm fifty," she told him. "And by then I'll know better."

"What did you do with the ring?" he asked out of the clear blue.

"I told you that's very personal and . . ."

"I know, this is business," he finished for her. "I

thought we were getting to be at least fairly decent friends."

"We are," she said. "But not best friends, Carson. And I don't want to talk about it."

Chapter Six

The rain started few hours before daybreak, and Molly roused enough to think about zipping her windows shut, but it sounded so peaceful and pleasant that she just shut her eyes and went back to sleep. In ten minutes it was coming down in great sheets, complete with lightning and thunder, and the plastic liner on the bottom of the tent began to leak. She sat up with a start. The sleeping bag began gathering more and more water. She unzipped the side, slid out of the bag and grabbed it up to hold over her head as she ran for the truck.

She reached up to undo the back tailgate and felt someone's hand brush her shoulder. Carson opened the door and picked her up from the waist and set her down inside the bed of the truck. Then he hopped in beside her and pulled the doors shut. "Whew." He opened a duffel bag and pulled out the last two clean towels he'd brought. "Here, use this to dry your hair," he said.

"Where did that all come from? Is it going to wash out tents away?" She attacked her long hair with the towel right after she used it to dry the water from her arms and legs. "Look at my feet. They look like I've been wallowing in mud."

"Get your hair dry, and then use the towel to get them clean." He followed his own advice. "You want to change clothes?"

"I'd love to," she said, "but . . ." she looked around at the cramped space. Even though the tents were outside as well as the cooler and most of the cooking gear, it was still filled with duffel bags and suitcases.

"Hey, I'll turn around and face the back," he chuckled. "Then you can do the same. I surely do not want to sit here all day in wet clothing."

"All day?" she moaned.

"Well . . ." He cleaned the mud off one foot, then had an idea. "I'm going back out," he said. "I'll get the cooler and cooking stuff and hand it to you. You can get it organized and put it back where it belongs while I take down the tents. They'll be wet but when we get them out tonight we can dry them off. See that window right there?" He pointed to the back window. "It slides. Think you could get all dry and skinny through that space?"

"I suppose I could but . . ."

"Hey, if we load up our stuff and can get into the cab, then we can simply drive out of here. If we can outrun the rain then we'll be back on course. If we can't then we'll find a laundromat and play catch up, then . . ."

"Sounds like a good plan to me." She was suddenly aware of how she must look with dripping hair and a wet night shirt.

Carson literally dodged lightning bolts with a prayer and a promise that if he got back inside the truck one more time, he'd never make such a foolhardy plan again in his lifetime. Molly organized the back end of the truck to accommodate the partially folded tents and everything else. Then she scooted over to make room for Carson when he crawled back inside, dripping wet from the top of his dark brown hair to his toes.

"Okay, here's a semi-dry towel," she tossed him the one he'd been using before he got back out in the weather. "Sorry, I didn't think to bring anything like towels. I just figured we'd stay in motels and we wouldn't need them." She fished around in her suitcase for clean underpants and a bra. "Now, turn around and let me get dressed."

He flipped his body around to face the back of the truck and watched the rain and lightning. His mind did crazy things as he listened to her moan when her head hit the roof as she tried to pull her shorts up over her still damp thighs. "Think we'll have a storm like this when we go to Africa?" he asked.

"If we do they'll probably pay us big bucks just to come back for the rain. They may think we're gods or something." She finally got the T-shirt over the top of her head. It was really quite warm in the back of the truck, but the noise of the constant, driving rain beating down on the top of the metal made her shiver. "Your turn now," she slipped through the window into the front seat of the truck.

She used the rearview mirror to fix her hair and found that she could see him from the chest up as he used the towel to dry off. But before she fully realized she was actually staring at him, he looked up and winked. "Hey, no fair," he called out. "I didn't have a mirror to watch you."

"Oh, hush, I'm fixing my hair," she snipped blushing.

"And a real blush," he taunted further as he popped a white T-shirt over his head. "I didn't know women still knew how to do that."

"Get dressed and hush," she commanded. Of course, she could still blush and had many times since they left Texas. She'd just been careful he didn't catch her or else he would know he had that kind of power over her.

"If you adjust the mirror just slightly, you can watch me put the rest of my clothes on," he continued to tease.

She turned the mirror all the way up so she couldn't see him at all, picked up her purse from the floor where she left it at night, and took out a small compact. But it took every ounce of her willpower to keep from turning it to an angle where she could see him.

He slithered through the window and surprised her with his agility. He wiggled down into the seat and pulled the truck keys from his pocket. "Shoulda just threw them over the seat," he mumbled. "Not so smart, sticking them down in my pocket then having to fish them out."

"At least you didn't leave them outside on the table and have to go get them. Thank goodness you remembered to put my computer away. I would have probably left it sitting on the table." She rolled her eyes.

"You are quite welcome," he smiled. "Now, let's see if we can drive out of here or if we're going to need a boat."

"If it doesn't stop we may need an ark," she moaned. "We're going to lose a whole day because of this."

"Well, so what." He could hardly believe she really complained. "We're ahead of schedule, and there were three or four days thrown in in case of bad weather or car trouble or anything else."

"Par . . . doon me." She wiggled her head and glared at him.

"Yes, ma'am." He put the truck in gear and eased out onto the paved road leading out of the campground. "Just that I didn't think anything could make you complain."

"Thank you," the glare turning to a twinkle. "I shall take that as a compliment. Now find us a McDonald's, please, kind chauffeur, and we shall dine on sausage biscuits. Then it would be really nice to find a laundromat. Besides towels, which you so graciously brought along, I'm running low on clothes. And it wouldn't hurt while we're at it to toss our sleeping bags in. They'll smell all musty if we don't."

They bought breakfast at a Hardee's and ate it in the truck, since the rain was still pouring down in buckets. Steak biscuits and coffee, which they both declared was truly murdered water in the first degree. When they pulled out onto the main street of the little town they'd found, there was a laundromat just across the street.

"Now if only they had a curbside window," she muttered as Carson backed the truck up close to the door.

"But they don't," he said. "So we'll dodge the rain-drops and do the best we can. Remember, when we're in Africa we'll remember this rain and wish for a downpour just like this."

"I'm so sure." She opened the door and trotted to the back of the truck, where he was already tossing an olive green duffel bag filled with towels and his dirty laundry. She grabbed a plastic garbage sack of her own things, and the two of them jogged across the sidewalk into the Speedy Laundromat. Sparkling white tile covered the floor, and the folding tables were covered with white Formica. Two women—one a tall blonde, the other an older lady with lavender hair—had a couple of dryers tied up. But all the washers were empty. Carson found enough quarters in his pocket to plug into three, and then dumped his duffel bag in the middle of the floor and started sorting clothes. Towels in one pile. White clothing in another and colors in a third. "Well, what are you waiting for, Molly? Ain't no sense in paying double. Towels will take a whole load, but you can put your whites in with mine and our colors can go together."

She nodded. To him it was just laundry, but dumping her underpants and bras on the floor and tossing them in with his jockey briefs and T-shirts was the hardest, most personal thing she'd done since she left home. She picked up the whites, more to keep him from coming into direct contact with her intimate things than anything, and pushed them into the nearest washer while he loaded one right beside it with towels.

"Soap?" she said. "I've got some change. I'll get it out of that machine over there." She slipped three quarters into the dispenser and a mini-sized carton of Cheer fell out the bottom. "Do you use bleach?"

"Nope, can't handle the stuff on my sensitive skin." He almost blushed and she laughed.

"Don't tell me Mr. Macho has a sensitive cell in his body," she bantered.

"Hello." The tall blonde angled up to his side. "I can tell by your accent you're not from around here."

Wow, Molly thought, *no kidding. What gave you the first clue, Sherlock?* She turned a faint shade of jealousy green as she eyed the woman in tight short shorts and a halter top. She wore some kind of tall, spongy platform sandals. If Carson didn't back away by the time the washing was finished, he would have to have her surgically removed. Someone had said Yankees were cold and unfriendly. Well, if that witch got any friendlier, they'd have to fight their way out of the Speedy Laundromat. And Molly didn't have a gun or anything to fight with . . . except the mini-box of Cheer. She might have to throw soap powder in her eyes and pull Carson away from her clutches.

"No we aren't." Carson was actually smiling at the Nordic goddess, who had a split between her front teeth wide enough to drive a Harley Davidson through.

"Well, where are you and your little sister from?" She shut her eyes, turned her head slowly toward Molly, and reopened them, as if looking down on a third-grade student who'd just failed a spelling test. Molly kept stuffing a third washer full of their clothing and tried to ignore the rudeness. Surely if two people joined their laundry, then other people should back off and leave them alone.

"She's not my sister, but we're from Texas," Carson

said, wondering why Molly looked like she could chew up pine trees and spit out toothpicks.

"Oh, and what is someone as good-looking as you doing up here in New York all the way from Texas?" The woman flicked a piece of lint from his shoulder.

"Getting hustled, evidently," Molly said loudly, and pulled herself up to her full height.

"You married to this hunk?" the woman asked. "If you are, honey, then start putting all your clothes in one basket. If not, then step back, because I'm the queen of hustling and I see something I want." She touched Carson's arm.

Molly almost let her have him. She came within a gnat's eyelash of saying she'd wait in the truck, letting him find his own way out of the maze. But the quizzical look in his eye dared her, and she didn't take challenges lying down. Granny had told her lots of times that life wasn't to be taken in a vertical position. Spit in its eye and whip its butt, but don't let it outdo you.

"Well, darlin', this is not your lucky day." Molly picked up the woman's hand from Carson's shoulder and dropped it like so much garbage as she slipped in between them. "We just spent part of our honeymoon in Niagara Falls, and we're on our way back home."

The woman set her jaw in disbelief and for a moment, Molly thought she really was going to have to fight her way out of the laundry. And she'd left her soap powder sitting on the washer, out of her reach.

"Well, then you better take care of him, little girl," the blonde said with a toss of the head. "I ever catch him in my territory again, he's mine." She picked up a basket of clothes and ran through the rain to a big, white Lincoln parked at the curb beside their truck.

"Thought for a minute there you were going to let me drown." He wiped his brow in an imaginary sweep with the back of his hand.

"I should have, probably," she mumbled. "I thought Yankees were unfriendly and cold as ice. I sure wouldn't want to see a hot, friendly one."

The little lady in the corner chuckled. "We are mostly just that," she said. "You will have to overlook Tasha. She's the resident bad girl. Always on the prowl and don't care what she has to do to get whatever man takes her eye. I hear you say you're from Texas. Now what are you doing up here all the way from Texas? Are you really on your honeymoon?"

"Excuse me, I've got to get the bedrolls and get them started, or we'll be here all day," Carson said as he trotted out to the truck, leaving Molly to explain her way out of the situation.

"No, we aren't. We're doing a photojournalism shoot for a tour company. From Texas to Canada to Niagara Falls and back down through Pennsylvania and then back west to Texas again," she explained to the elderly lady with the softest brown eyes set in a full, unwrinkled face.

"Well, honey, you play your cards just right and you

could make it a honeymoon. Feller there is sure enough taken with you," she whispered.

"Oh, why would you say that?" Molly whispered back as Carson opened the door, lugging in two soaked bedrolls.

"Just trust an old woman's sixth sense," she said behind her hand. "Plain as daylight. Nice meeting you. Have a safe journey home." She pulled the rest of her clothes from a dryer and toted them out the front door to a bright blue compact car.

Molly picked up a tattered *Redbook* from a rack at the end of the folding table and found a chair in front of the washers. That made three people who thought they were newlyweds. Not one time in all the months she'd been engaged to Darrin did anyone mention how he looked at her. And now, in a land of complete strangers noted for their aloofness, three different people had suggested such a thing.

She opened the book to an article on redecorating the bedroom and pretended to read while she listened to the rhythm of the rain as it lightened up and fell against the glass storefront. Her heart was still in limbo from Darrin and would be until she got home and found out where he actually stood on the matter. A few weeks of thinking about his asinine assumptions might make him realize just what a fool he'd been. But where did she stand on the matter? Right then, as she looked at the pictures in the book, she didn't know.

Carson picked up an old *National Geographic* and thumbed through it. He smiled when he thought about how she'd stepped right in between him and the hustler. There was an article on bald eagles and he remembered her comment on the hawk he caught in flight with the setting sun as a backdrop. Would either of them ever be so fortunate as to meet the editor of this great magazine? If he were offered a job at a remote place, he would ask her to go with him to do the writing end, and just that thought rattled his brain for several minutes. But he still had no doubt if she were offered the same position, she surely wouldn't make it contingent upon him taking the photographs for her.

Carson thumbed through a picture book about the Civil War in the middle of the bookstore, keeping Molly in his peripheral vision. She was in the mystery section, picking up first a paperback of John Sandford's and then one by an author he had only recently heard about, someone by the name of Randy Wayne White.

They'd finished their laundry in silence, grabbing the hot clothes from the piles to fold as soon as the dryers stopped turning. He'd folded clothes often with his sisters, and women's things didn't embarrass him one bit, but he could tell by the way Molly jerked her underpants and bras away and folded them, hurriedly stuffing them in her duffel bag, that it did embarrass her. So he didn't make jokes—rather just methodically folded every piece and put them back into the truck.

It was still raining when they left the laundromat, and it continued to do so all the way south through New York. He wondered what she'd write about that state, and was glad he'd at least gotten a few pictures last night. The sunset, a few of an old scraggly tree with buzzards sitting in its branches, and one of a pond surrounded with cat-o-nine tails.

"Any ideas? We're not going to have a lot if we just drive through it in the rain," he said.

"Next exit says there's a shopping mall. I hate to shop, but it might have a bookstore and a food court. We could hole up there for a few hours and see what the weather does," she offered.

"You hate to shop?" He couldn't believe his ears.

"Yes, I hate to shop. Granny fusses at me, too. But it seems like such a worthless pastime. If I've got time to waste, I'd rather read or cook or anything but chase through clothing stores. If I need something, I go look for it until I find that item, buy it, and go home."

"I see," he said. *Wow!* He thought.

"This exit?"

"Yes, and there's the mall. It's slacked off a little, so we might not even get wet," she said. "Beat you to the front door. Winner buys the loser dinner."

He started off in a dead run and was already touching the door before he realized just how she'd phrased the stakes. "That was pretty lowdown," he said when she jogged up to his side.

"Yep, but it worked. And you're in luck. I'm not very hungry. How about pizza? I can only eat a couple of medium-sized ones." She laughed at the look on his face.

So they ate pizza, still without talking much, and went to the bookstore, where he was half wishing he could have been there in the Civil War and taken some of the pictures he saw in the book. Molly could have been beside him . . . *oh, no she couldn't,* he argued with himself. *She would have been a woman then as well as now and in those days you wouldn't be traipsing all over God's great green earth with her. She would have been home learning needlepoint and rolling bandages for the soldiers.*

"Not Molly. She would have spit in their eye," he mumbled.

"What?" she whispered.

"Nothing." He shook his head. "Just wondering about what kind of camera they used to take these old black-and-white pictures."

"Probably a tintype thing," she looked over his shoulder. "Pretty gruesome, wasn't it?" She reached out and touched a photo of a young man, dark-haired, very dead, and brushed Carson's fingertips. The shock was still there, but it didn't amaze her anymore. Some people were just attracted to each other and there wasn't a thing anyone could do about it. But professional people learned to control their baser instincts and work together. Professional . . . that's all she and Carson would ever be.

Chapter Seven

The journey of a lifetime starts with a tiny step, someone once said. A lifetime begins with a journey . . . of the heart . . . and often ends before a tiny step gets taken. So it seemed to Molly that day. The last day of the trip. They'd crossed Missouri and could be back in Texas in the wee hours of the morning. But they'd discussed how they would spend the last day a couple of nights before when they camped out in Indianapolis and decided the last night would be the one they splurged on.

"Why don't we stop at the most expensive, biggest hotel in the area. One with a heated indoor pool, a Jacuzzi, free full breakfast bar, and even an exercise room?" she suggested as they fished that night in the creek running through the campground. The cheapest one so far—only ten dollars each. They'd shared supper chores. She made the fry-bread and spicy meat for Indian tacos, while he cut up lettuce, tomatoes, and cheese.

"Sounds like a great plan to me. We can pack all the gear and not even have to unpack on the final night. We've saved a wad of money, and if I'm careful I can stay out of that sportswriter's job for a little while longer, while I wait for my ship to come in." He watched his red and white bobble take a dive in the water. But when he reeled the catch in, all he found on his hook was a medium-sized turtle.

"Texas," she sounded wistful.

"Homesick?" he asked.

"Probably will be every time I leave home. Can't wait to drink good old Texas water and breathe Texas air, but I'll always keep a suitcase ready to pack. Kind of like a bittersweet thing. Homesick when I'm away and antsing to go all the time," she said.

They checked into a hotel in Springfield, Missouri. It had all the prerequisite features they'd already discussed, but it really was a bit of a bittersweet experience for Molly to unload her suitcase in the room. Two weeks on the road and she'd grown to like working with Carson in the makeshift kitchen at the close of the day, to enjoy discussing the books they were both reading and to even ask for a word now and then when she couldn't find the right one to fit what she wanted to say.

She soaked in a real tub with real bubbles made from the little bottle of complimentary shampoo in a basket on the vanity, wrapped herself in a big, fluffy bathrobe with the hotel initials embroidered on the lapel, and threw herself down on the bed. Half an hour to rest, and then they were going to some fancy joint to eat. They'd seen it advertised in a brochure they picked up when they crossed the line. And they were going there on the river in motorboat. Then they had reservations to eat on the deck overlooking the shoreline.

She couldn't possibly lie still, so she bounced out of bed and hooked up the iron which was another complimentary luxury, ". . . which I'm sure I paid for dearly when I gave them all that money," she mumbled to herself as she shook out a sundress from the duffel bag. She'd brought two cotton dresses and they'd spent the whole trip wadded up in a ball at the bottom of her suitcase. She chose the floral one, with big Hawaiian-looking flowers scattered all over the fitted bodice and the long skirt of flowing rayon. It wasn't hard to press, and in just a few minutes she was twisting her hair up into a French knot, which she held in place with a big red plastic clamp.

"I look like I've been set down in bougainvillea and a tropical fish got tangled in my hair," she muttered to the mirror as she applied lip liner and mascara.

She had barely finished when she heard a gentle knock on the door and opened it to find Carson decked out in starched and ironed jeans, perfect creases running up the legs from the bunched up bottoms over his polished black boots, to the silver belt buckle and onto the crisp white shirt.

"Where did all that come from?" she asked in awe.

"Same place that lovely dress did, I'm sure," he smiled.

"You iron?" She was truly amazed.

"Of course. Momma said just because I was a boy didn't mean I didn't have to learn all the arts. Cooking, cleaning, ironing, washing dishes, and dusting. The girls had to take out trash, mow the lawn, start up the weed eater, and even bait their own hook when we fished. She said there wasn't any gender gaps in our family. Daddy could make supper and she could plow a field as good as he could," Carson leaned against the door jamb.

"Smart woman. Sounds a lot like my granny," she said, stopping to pick up her thin evening bag.

"You look beautiful. Got your room key?" he asked.

"Thank you and yes," she held up the plastic card before shoving it inside her purse. "Now lead the way to the restaurant. I'm going to eat until my fat cells wallow in ecstasy."

"What fat cells?" He almost slipped his arm around her shoulders, but stopped himself just in time.

"Oh, I've got them. After the breakfasts and suppers we've eaten for the past two weeks, I'm surprised I can even wiggle into my bathing suit," she said as she pushed the button for the elevator to take them to the ground floor.

"Didn't look so bad in it last time we swam," he said, meaning every word.

"Thank you again, but flattery will get you nowhere. I don't trust men in general, and especially those who look as handsome as you do tonight," she told him when they were in the close quarters of the elevator. He inhaled deeply and loved that wonderful light scent she used. He entertained a fleeting vision of the elevator sticking between floors. What a tragedy to get stuck for a couple of hours with Molly, who looked like a Hawaiian princess from the top of her jet black hair all the way to her bright red sandals.

"So what are you ordering?" she asked, looking over the mouth-watering menu and wishing she could sample everything there. The night air was pleasant for a summer night, but not nearly cool enough to raise goose bumps on her bare shoulders. The breeze brought the smell of the river water to the deck where she and Carson were the only patrons at that time of the evening.

"It's one shell of a place," Molly quoted, reading the inscription at the top of the menu. "Crawfish. That's what I want. The big order. Salad with my meal instead of before and French fries."

"What can I get you to drink?" a waitress appeared at their table and she even sounded almost like the people in Texas. Not quite the soft drawl but closer than the sweet little black lady in the laundromat in New York who kept saying you instead of ya'll.

"Sweet tea with lemon," Carson said.

"Same here," Molly said.

"Ready to order?" she asked.

Molly told her exactly what she wanted. Carson ordered the steak and surf: lobster and KC strip, done rare, with a salad, also served with his meal instead of before. Molly stared out across the river at the trees and the mountain on the other side. Branson wasn't far away with all the shows and tourists, but a person would never know it as they sat on the deck of this place and waited for their dinner to arrive. She felt like a southern belle sipping a mint julep . . . only it was lemon-spiked tea. But a southern lady in the days of mint juleps wouldn't be traveling around unchaparoned with a gentleman. And Carson had truly been a gentleman through the weeks. They'd managed to make the trip, like the professor said, in spite of gender, and they'd done a bang-up good job of it, too. Even if she did have her doubts in the beginning, when she wanted to strangle him most of the time.

"Ever eaten crawfish?" he finally asked. He'd been watching her expressions change as she studied the gentle river and scenery. One time she cocked her head to the side and fluttered her eyes ever so gently. Anyone else wouldn't have caught the slight mannerism, but Carson had studied Molly for two weeks, and he knew she must be thinking about another time and place. He wondered if she was telling Darrin just what she thought about him when she did that.

"Crawfish," she shook her head. "Nope, never have. But Granny did one time and she told me they were wonderful. I can't wait to try them."

"Going to eat them the real Cajun style?" His brown eyes glittered with mischief.

"What's that?" she asked.

"You pop the tails off, dip them in red sauce and then suck the brains out of the critter," he said, expecting her to shiver.

"Sure, that's the way Granny said she learned to eat them." She nodded seriously.

"You are kidding me," he said.

"Why would I do that? Isn't that the way everyone eats crawfish?"

"But . . ." He started to argue and she pointed an imaginary gun at him with her forefinger and thumb. "Bang, I got you," she said. "Of course I'm not going to suck the brains out of them. Eating the tails won't bother me one bit because that's just like shrimp, but sucking brains . . ." She shivered and wrapped her arms around her middle.

"I believed you." He laughed out loud. "I wonder how many other lies you've told me in the past few days."

"Keep 'em guessing." She pretended she was putting her fantasy pistol in a holster on her hip. "Here comes our food. Would you like me to save you the critter's brains? I won't toss them out if you want them. I wouldn't think of being selfish."

"No, thank you. I think this lobster tail and steak will take care of my fat cells just fine," he told her.

"Fat cells, hmmp," she said. "You've got less than I do."

"Thank you, kind madam, for that and the compliment about me being handsome a while ago. I did hear it. Thought you'd never notice, though." He was flirting and she was tongue-tied. This was the last night. Friendship—maybe, after all they'd been through, especially the situation with the blonde hustler in the laundry and enduring that miserable rain most of the way through the state of New York, and then trying to write something enticing. Carson told her she could write a humorous essay about the tall blonde but she just shot him a mean look, which made him roar with laughter.

"You are quite welcome." She nodded seriously and picked up the first crawfish with her fingers, popped the tail off, peeled it back, found the succulent flesh inside, and dug it out. She dipped it in the red sauce, put it in her mouth, and forgot all about flirting. Maybe she'd ask for an assignment to the Florida Keys when she got to be a real journalist, and eat crawfish every single night.

Just inches separated them as they rode home in the motorboat, but it might as well have been miles. He couldn't think of a thing to say except that the water was gorgeous with the moon and stars reflected in it, and that he should have brought along a camera. She just nodded.

"Where you two from?" the driver of the boat asked when several moments had passed with nothing but silence. Usually the people he ferried back and forth were loquacious and sometimes even a bit loud-mouthed. This young couple looked like they'd just been to a funeral rather than an expensive night out on the river.

"Texas," Molly expected him to ask if they were on their honeymoon.

"Big place," he said, but that's as far as it went.

"Okay," Carson parked the truck at the hotel. This wasn't going to be a night of sadness—not if he had a say-so in the matter. "I'll race you to the elevators and then give you five minutes to get into your bathing suit. Then we're going to the hot tub and when we're all relaxed, we'll take advantage of their swimming pool. Nothing is free, and we paid dearly for all these goodies."

"I can beat you to the elevators." She eyed him closely with a giggle of relief. She slipped her feet out of the sandals and left them lying in the truck, opened the door, and was off before he could even get the truck locked.

"You're cheating," he called.

"But I'm winning," she yelled over her shoulder. "If you're not here when the doors open, I'm not waiting on you either."

He threw out his hand and kept the doors open but he was panting for all he was worth, and bent over, putting his hands on his knees as he tried to catch his breath. "You . . . are . . . a . . . brazen one!" he said.

"And . . . you . . . are . . . a . . . slowpoke." She worked at filling her lungs as hard as he did.

"Thought I was in better shape," he said when the doors opened and he was somewhere between breathing normal and panting. "Too much riding. Not enough running."

"You jog?" she asked, afraid to try too many words at once.

"Every day, usually," he nodded. "Two weeks without it and look at me."

"Me, too. We should've been making laps around the camps." She was elated she could speak a whole sentence.

"Meet you downstairs at the hot tub in ten minutes?" He paused at the door.

She just nodded, slipped her plastic card in the door, waited for the green light, and disappeared before he even noticed she wasn't wearing shoes. She fell onto the bed in a heap and inhaled deeply several times. So much for melancholy. That's one thing she did like about having Carson for a friend. He wasn't a pessimist and always kept things going.

She dug around in her bag until she came up with a bright red-and-white-striped bikini, not the usual solid, black one-piece bathing suit she had been wearing. She stripped out of her dress, put the bikini on along with a white cover-up, and was in the elevator on her way down to the pool room when she realized she was flirting. Maybe not with words but most definitely with the bikini. She pushed the button to go back up when the elevator stopped, but then on impulse stepped out. He flirted. Probably because I'm the only woman he's been around except the New York hustler, but he did flirt, so I'm not going back up and change my suit.

Carson leaned back in the tub and shut his eyes. After that quiet episode in the boat, she might change her mind and send a message down telling him she was going to sleep. The hot water eased the muscles in his neck and back, and he didn't even know he'd been tense. When he opened his eyes she was beside the tub and he gasped sharply and hoped she didn't hear it. She was taking the familiar bathing suit cover off, the one she wore lots of times when they swam at night, but underneath it wasn't the usual black suit. There was a red and white bikini and a perfect body for it.

"Dive right in, honey, the water is fine," he found his voice hiding somewhere back behind a tonsil.

"Looks hot," she stepped in gingerly.

"Little bit," he nodded, "but real good for aching muscles weary from traveling all these days."

She eased her whole body down into the water and sighed. This was as close to heaven as she wanted to be for a while. Someday when she had her own house she was going to invest in one of these things and make sure she got her money out of it every day. "Do you feel a little like we're being cooked for some kind of canabalistic ritual? Any minute someone is going to turn up the heat, and a bunch of half-naked people are going to come in here with spears and dance around the tub, chanting and eyeing our fingers and toes."

"Why our fingers and toes?" he asked with a chuckle.

"That's the succulent parts," she said. "Take a long time to cook our liver and . . ."

"Hush." He shivered. "Where do you get that horrid imagination of yours?"

"It's what makes good journalism." She laughed. "Didn't know you were squeamish after all that talk of sucking brains out of crawfish. Tell me, do you eat calf fries?"

"No, I've never been that hungry." He snarled his nose at the very thought of such delicacies.

"Me, either," she said. "I'm glad we're not calling it a night, Carson. I want to stay up and play and then sleep late tomorrow. Checkout isn't until noon."

"Then we shall leave at noon. We'll be home by dark even then," he said. "How much longer are we going to chance liver damage by sitting in this hot water?"

"I don't think we have anything to worry about just yet." She pressed her forefinger into his upper arm. That silly sensation was still there, but it didn't surprise her nearly as much as the first time when he put a piece of cheese in her mouth. "You're not even beginning to get well done on the outside. It would take all night to boil your liver."

"Yuk." He made a face, the dimple in the side of his cheek deepened.

She leaned back and shut her eyes, enjoying the warmth and not even caring what Carson did right then. He could stay or go away . . . just so long as he didn't go too far. Half an hour later she awoke with a start to find him staring intently at her. "Guess it is relaxing," she yawned.

"You snored," he said.

"I do not snore," she snipped.

"You did then," he said. "An old couple came in and joined us for a little while, but they whispered so they wouldn't wake you. The blue-haired lady said you looked tired and that our honeymoon must be wearing you out."

"Carson, did they really?" Her blue eyes widened out.

He pulled his imaginary gun from his holster and fanned back the thumb trigger.

"Paybacks are not pleasant."

"Oh, hush." She had to laugh. "Let's go swim. I'm all napped out and ready to play."

She bounced twice on the diving board and dived into the water with the grace of a ballet dancer. He just did a half-hearted jump from the side of the pool and met her at the other end. She dived beautifully but her swimming strokes left a lot to be desired. He could never dive worth a flip, literally, but his strokes were beautiful.

She beat him to the end but she churned the water as she went. She was amazed at his form when she turned to watch him approach. "Mercy, where'd you learn to do that?"

"I don't know." He blushed at the compliment.

"You're really good. You could do that Olympic stuff. I don't think you even made a splash." She leaned her arms back and braced them on the edge of the pool.

"But I don't want to do that. I want to take pictures and . . ." He stopped and did the same thing. Leaned back and kicking his feet just slightly in the shallow end of the pool.

A short, stocky lady with blue hair done in a kinky-do that defied all laws of gravity and a bald-headed man opened the door to the pool room. She wore a two-piece bathing suit from the 1940s in navy blue with white piping. One of those boy-cut, short bottoms and a top that covered everything. Only three inches of midriff showed, and the elderly gentleman had his arm around that middle and patted her as if he was afraid she'd disappear.

"Hi." The lady eased into the shallow end with his help and he stepped in behind her. "We thought we might be the only ones here." Her green eyes glittered.

"Hello," Molly said. "We were just leaving."

"Oh, don't let us run you off. This is just our ritual swim. We went to Niagara Falls fifty years ago on our honeymoon, and when we were driving home to Guyman, Oklahoma, we stopped in this town. They didn't have indoor pools in those days, but we did find a new modern motel that had one out back, and we went swimming. Our very first time in a real pool. We usually swam in the creeks. So we went swimming and now we come back here every year and do our ritual swim . . . in the same bathing suits," she chattered on.

"But we were really just leaving. We've got a long day ahead of us tomorrow." Molly cut her eyes around at Carson. "Weren't we?"

"Yes, of course," he said.

"Well, here it is, Momma," the older gentleman said. "A picture of before and after. Here we are after fifty years, three kids, eight grandchildren, and a couple of great-grands. And there they are just beginning. They've got better things to do on their honeymoon than sit and listen to stories from a couple of old codgers like us. Where you kids from?" he asked.

"Texas," Molly couldn't help but blush and Carson adored the high color in her cheeks.

"Come all the way from Texas to Missouri? Why, you could've gone to Houston," the lady said. "But come back every year and bring that pretty red bathing suit, honey. It keeps 'em in line, you know. Kind of romantic to put on the same one each year and fall in love all over again," she winked.

"Yes, ma'am," Molly said.

"There's pay-per-view on the television," he said as they waited one more time for the elevator. "Want to split the cost of a movie?"

"My place or yours," she asked.

"Are you flirting with me, Molly Baker?" he asked.

"Business. Totally business," she said seriously. "If it's my place I need five minutes to pick up my personal things laying all over the floor."

"Then my place, by all means," he said.

"Give me five minutes to change into my shorts and T-shirt," she said.

"I thought you looked pretty good in that outfit," he said.

"Carson Rhodes, are you flirting with me?" she challenged.

"Business. Purely business," he shot right back.

He sat in a recliner beside the end table and she stretched out on the king-sized bed, her feet toward the headboard, her chin propped up in her hands. "What are we watching?"

"*Armageddon,*" he said. "I haven't seen it yet and it's the best choice we've got."

"Good, I haven't seen it either," she told him.

Two hours later tears were streaming down her face. She didn't even care if he heard her sobbing when the credits rolled at the end of the movie. She'd laughed and sighed and then broke down in tears, and somehow she didn't know if she was crying just because of the movie or if she just needed a good weeping session to clean out her soul.

"I'm sorry." She grabbed a tissue from the night stand and brushed his hand as he reached for one, too. He blew his nose and it sounded like a foghorn, and she followed it with her elephant blast. "I'm sorry," she apologized again. "I never did learn to blow my nose or sneeze like a lady."

"It's okay," he said around the baseball-size lump in his throat. "Want to watch it again?"

"Maybe in fifty years on my honeymoon." Her chin quivered and another bout of tears were in the making down deep in her heart.

"Want me to walk you to your room?"

"It's right next door and there's not a Texas-sized booger man coming at earth right now," she said as she pulled out a couple more tissues and wiped her eyes.

"Meet you at noon at the truck then." He didn't want her to leave but couldn't ask her to stay. She still didn't talk about Darrin, and there was always the possibility she was harboring a great love and greater hurt in that area. And besides, like she'd said, it was business. Purely business.

But someone sure forgot to tell his heart.

Molly threw her shorts and shirt on the chair beside her bed and pulled her faithful old knit nightshirt over her head. She fluffed up the pillows and fell into bed but didn't go right to sleep. What would she do if tomorrow was the last day? If the big boom came? Would she, in her journalistic capacity, be there with her mini-recorder which she had left laying on her bed in Bells, Texas? Or would she forget all about that and spend the precious hours in a personal way?

She finally went to sleep, but she didn't have any answers. She just knew that somewhere down deep in her heart when she thought about the end, she knew she'd want Carson Rhodes beside her. It was as unsettling to her soul as the movie had been to her heart.

Chapter Eight

Carson took a few pictures of the Oklahoma countryside as they drove that last day, but not as many as he had taken the first day they covered part of the same territory. When she asked him if he was anxious to get back home, he just said that when the tourists were on the final leg of the journey, they wouldn't be interested in their worn-out travel log any more. They might be thinking about all the fun they had, but they'd also be thinking about what they were going to tell their friends and if the tomatoes were in bloom or if the cow had birthed that calf since they'd left.

"What about you, Carson?" she asked in the middle of the afternoon when they stopped in Henrietta at McDonalds for a hamburger. "You thinking about a calf or the tomatoes?"

"Nope." He dipped a French fry in his paper container of catsup. "I'm thinking about getting these pictures developed so I can see what I got. I'm holding my breath that they all look as good in reality as they did through the lens."

"You mean you've got doubts?" she asked.

"Of course. Don't you have a little niggling doubt about what you wrote? You hope it will be just what the boss wants, so good the editor doesn't even have to add a comma, but isn't there just a little fear that they'll chop the devil out of it so bad you won't even recognize your own work?"

"Yes, there is," she said. "Actually I'm scared to death we won't pass this big test thing the professor keeps talking about. Do you think it's something written? Or if it's just whether or not the company is pleased with our package?"

"Who knows?" He rolled his eyes. "With Professor Johnson it might be whether or not we wear ironed or unironed jeans."

"I didn't know Troy Aikman was from here." She changed the subject abruptly when she noticed all the memorabilia on the walls. "This place is a shrine to him."

"Seems that way," he said. "Reckon they'll ever hang everything you ever wore or touched at some restaurant in Bells, Texas?"

"Oh, sure," she said. "They'll put my red bikini behind glass and the first essay I ever wrote in the third grade about how ugly grasshoppers were."

"Grasshoppers?" He raised an eyebrow.

"Yes, I'm terrified of them. They've got big horrid eyeballs and they feel like Velcro when they touch you, and Noah should have let the other animals eat them or step on them." She shuddered.

"But they make wonderful fish bait, and you baited your own hook with a worm and they are slippery and slimy," he countered.

"They are not grasshoppers. I would not voluntarily touch a grasshopper for anything," she declared.

"Not even for that job in Africa? There are grass-hoppers there, I'm sure. You'd give up that assignment because you don't like grasshoppers?" he asked.

She thought about it for a moment, setting her mouth in a firm line and drawing her eyebrows down. It was a hard decision, one that would take lots of weighing the pros and cons. "How long do I have to make up my mind?"

"Oh, take all the time you want, Miss Baker. We only have an airplane on hold with the propeller already spinning. So you've got five minutes to pack your suitcase or we'll ask Miss Atkins if she would like to go." He rubbed his chin in mock seriousness.

"Beth Atkins! Why did you mention her?"

"She just came to mind." He could tell he'd touched a raw nerve. Right here within hours of getting home, and he'd made her mad. Surely it wasn't jealousy. Because to be jealous she would have to care about him, and she'd not given even an inch in that area. Professional. Purely professional.

"But she's . . ." She crammed her Big Mac in her mouth and bit off a huge chunk to keep from saying anything hateful. Beth was the prettiest student in the whole graduate program. She had a fairly good eye for photography and wasn't too shabby a writer, either. And she was always flitting around Carson. It wasn't any secret that she'd like to wrap her long arms around him and carry him off to a foreign island for a lifetime.

"She's what?" He pursued the subject.

"She's not about to go to Africa." She talked around the food in her mouth until she could get it swallowed. "It's my dream and my job, and I'll battle the grass-hoppers before I let her steal it out from under my nose."

"Well said, Molly Baker." He put his food down and clapped for her.

"Thank you." She bowed and almost got her long black hair in her hamburger.

She curled up with her pillow propped up against the door and went to sleep after lunch. She offered to take a turn driving, but he said he'd driven the whole trip and he'd finish the job. That had been their agreement in the beginning. She'd navigate with the maps and instructions from the company and he would drive, but it seemed only polite that she would at least ask if he'd like some relief, since they were so close to home and no navigation was necessary.

She had a nightmare about grasshoppers in her bed and awoke with a whimper, but just readjusted her position and went back to sleep. When they crossed the Red River into Texas she sat straight up. "Home," she said. "Never looked so good."

"Want to stop and get a free cup of coffee, maybe a road map and some brochures?" He slowed the truck down to get on the ramp taking them to the Texas welcome center.

"No, I don't, but keep going. I want a drink of pure old Texas water, and I do need to find a ladies room. You probably need to stretch your legs anyway, and now that I think about it, I want a candy bar from the vending machine and a Coke."

"Sleeping made you hungry, did it?"

"Something did. I had a nightmare about grasshoppers." She bailed out of the truck the minute it was parked. "Maybe that made me hungry."

"You want some chocolate-covered raisins. You can pretend they're grasshoppers," he teased.

"Not on your life," she yelled over her shoulder just before she opened the door to the restroom.

"So, what are they going to hang on the Mc-Donald's walls in Sherman when you make your mark in the world. I forgot to ask you back there when you started talking about Beth Atkins." She wiggled in her seat like a two-year-old as they got closer and closer to her home.

"Sherman? I didn't grow up in a big place like Sherman. I grew up in Van Alstyne. Now if they put all my things on the wall there, I'm sure they'll want my first camera, an Instamatic from Wal-Mart, and the first picture I ever shot. A good-looking photo of my dog, Jake. At least most of him. He jumped and all I got was his hind legs and tail."

"Jake? So you have a dog. Who's taking care of him? Did you leave him at your folks' place?"

"Is this personal or professional?" he taunted.

"Professional, of course. We're talking about your professional beginnings." She grinned and the flutter in his heart told him that he was going to miss her terribly when he awoke the next morning.

"Well, Jake died when I was fifteen. He was thirteen years old, and yes, I cried," he said.

"I'm sorry," she said soberly.

"Someday I'll show you my collection of Jake pictures. It's pretty impressive but then he was a pretty impressive subject," Carson told her.

"I'd like that," she said.

Granny was sitting in the porch swing when Carson drove up in the circular driveway just outside the yard fence. She shaded her eyes with her hand, wondering who in the world drove a red truck like that, then came off the porch like a banty rooster when she saw Molly getting out on the passenger's side.

"You're home." She patted her granddaughter's arm to be sure she was real.

"I told you two weeks, and it's exactly that today," Molly hugged her grandmother and introduced her to Carson, who was busy unloading Molly's equipment and suitcases from the back of the truck.

"But I didn't know what time," Hilda said. "I just knew it was today. Supper is on the stove. Red beans and fried potatoes. Cornbread and a platter of fried chicken. Carson, you want to stay?"

"Well . . ." He looked at Molly for his cue.

"Of course he does. We ate hamburgers a few hours ago, but he'll stay and eat some supper, won't you, Carson?" She grabbed his arm and pulled him toward the house.

"I guess you can twist my arm," he said.

"Okay." She wrenched his arm behind him so fast he didn't know what hit.

"Hey, that hurt."

"Of course it did, but now you can stay for supper and help me tell Granny all about what we saw. She's going to want a play-by-play, and I might miss something important like the turtle on the yellow line or those water towers marked hot, warm, and cold."

"Okay, okay." He laughed.

The house wasn't very big. A nice-sized living room with not a speck of dust anywhere. Pictures of

Molly everywhere. When she was a little girl in a white pinafore over a red dress. One of her in a pink ballet costume when she was in elementary school. As a teenager when her teeth were bigger than her face. Graduation cap and gown with her grandmother hugged up to her side. At some kind of award dinner when she was shaking hands with a professor.

"A shrine." She giggled when she noticed him trying to take in all the pictures in one glance. "Later, after I see all your pictures of Jake, then you can look at the ones of me. Right now, let's eat. You can sit right here." She motioned to him to sit at the head of the small table in the dining room. "And I'll sit here and Granny can have the other end."

Hilda was putting bright yellow place mats on the table, with matching napkins. Everything in the kitchen was either primary yellow or green, and even at dusk it felt as if sunshine was beaming through the windows. "Now sit right up to the table, son, and tell me, did she behave herself? She can be right snippy sometimes. Don't know where she gets it. From her Irish momma, I suppose," she said.

"Oh, sure, I get it straight from you," Molly said. "Like grandmother, like granddaughter. Here, Carson, help yourself." She passed him a platter of cornbread and then the bowl of pintos.

"Well, she did get hateful a few times, but we seemed to work fairly well together, on a purely professional level," he said without a hint of a grin.

"Oh?" Hilda stared straight at him without blinking.

"Yes, that's what she kept telling me, that we were working on a professional level," he said.

"I see," Hilda said. "Then tell me Mr. and Mrs. Professional Level just what all you saw and when the pictures are going to be ready."

It was ten o'clock that night before Carson and Molly got through filling Hilda in on all they'd done. Molly even told her about the brassy blonde in New York and the sweet little lady who told her that the woman was used to getting what she wanted. But she didn't tell her about the three or four different times that someone truly thought they were newlyweds. Carson took his cues from her and told about the rain and eating Mexican in Omaha and even the man who was playing the saxophone on the corner.

"And now I must thank you ladies for a truly scrumptious meal and take my tired old overstuffed bones home. It's only a few miles, but home is calling my name as much as it did yours, Molly," he said.

Hilda kicked her under the table and nodded toward the door. So Granny thought she'd better walk the fellow to the door. Well, that was one whale of a lot more than she ever wanted her to do with Darrin. She usually just yawned several times and said she was going to bed and for Molly to lock up when Darrin "finally went home."

"Molly, supper was delicious, and I thank you for

letting me stay." He crossed the porch toward his truck. "I'll call you tomorrow when I get the pictures done, and we'll get out your computer and polish up the package, if that's all right with you. I suppose we could just—"

"No, I want to see them." She shook her head. "I want to be sure I've captured the spirit with every line. Just call me and we'll decide where to spread the whole affair out and work on it."

"About six tomorrow evening, then?" he asked.

"You'll get them done that fast?"

"Oh, sure. I've got a deal with a photography place in Sherman. They do all my processing and they're pretty precise," he said.

"On Sunday?"

"Sure. I'll call at six, then. Maybe we could get together on Monday?"

"Sounds good to me, and give the whole package to the professor on Tuesday or Wednesday," she said.

"Well, see you then." He hated to turn around and leave her on the porch. He was used to watching her crawl into her tent and zip it up. Maybe if he went back and at least hugged her. Friends did that sometimes. He had lots of friends that he hugged when he said good-bye. So why was it so hard to make his feet take two steps back to the porch and just do it?

" 'Bye, Carson. It's been a wonderful trip." She put up one hand to wave.

"It sure has." He smiled and opened his truck door.

"Oh, Carson," she called out, and he turned.

"I gave the ring back because he said we weren't engaged anymore if I didn't stay home and not go with you. He said no woman of his was traipsing around the countryside with another man, no matter how professional it all was. He also said that once we were married that I was supposed to stay home and be a ranch wife," she said all in one breath and then wondered where in the devil it had all spilled out from.

"And waste all your talent?" He shook his head in bewilderment.

"Thank you," she said with only the faintest of smiles.

"Does that mean we're best friends now?" he asked, but he didn't wait for an answer. He just slammed the door and was gone before she could speak.

Chapter Nine

She chose a white suit with a short, straight skirt and a matching short-sleeved jacket to wear to church. She slipped her feet down into a pair of white leather shoes with three-inch boxy heels and fastened a gold chain with a tiny open heart charm hanging from it around her neck. It felt good to be dressed up after two weeks of jeans and T-shirts, and she was looking forward to seeing Brenda at church that morning.

She and Brenda had been friends since first grade, and the only time they'd been separated for more than a couple of days was right out of high school, when Brenda and Tom got married and she went to California for two weeks on her honeymoon. She had a three-year-old daughter, Kayla, and was six months' pregnant with her second child. She waited on the church lawn for Molly that morning.

"Oh," she said as she hugged Molly around her big, round protruding tummy. "I missed you so much. We've got to catch up. Come sit beside me." She pulled her friend away from Hilda and toward the church door. "Granny, we promise to be good." She giggled at Hilda's frown.

"You two don't know how to be good, and I'm tellin' you if I hear one, just one giggle from that back row, I'm going to fuss at both of you. Grown or not, you better be ladies in church." Hilda shook her finger at them.

"Yes, ma'am," Brenda said, smoothing down the front of her cranberry red maternity dress. Her blond hair was cut shoulder-length, and she wore it straight with feather bangs. She was three inches taller than Molly, and even when she wasn't pregnant she had to battle her weight constantly.

"So, what's going on?" Molly whispered when they slid into the pew beside Tom.

"It's Darrin," Brenda said. "He says you gave back the ring before you left."

"I did," Molly whispered.

The music director asked them to turn to hymn number 155 and Molly picked up the hymnal from the back of the pew in front of them. She turned to the right page and Brenda said, "Why? Does that mean you aren't getting married in September and I don't have to be skinny by then?"

"I guess so," Molly said.

Brenda started to say something else but the double doors at the back of the church opened wide and Darrin stood there in a black Western-cut suit, his blond hair combed back, his boots polished to a high shine, and Beth Atkins on his arm. She wore the exact same suit Molly had on. White short skirt, white jacket, and white shoes with a high, blocky heel. The only thing different was that she had a wide gold bangle bracelet and heavy herringbone gold chain around her neck. Her hair was piled high on her head, and she looked across the aisle straight into Molly's big blue eyes and gave her the slightest sneer of a smile.

It all happened in a fraction of a second, and then the doors were shut and Darrin led Beth to the middle of the church, where he sat with his parents. For the past six months he'd sat beside Molly in that same spot. Molly kept waiting for the tears to form on her eyelashes and spill out over her high cheekbones. Then she waited for the anger to boil up from her toenails to the top of her head. But neither one happened. The music director smiled at the latecomers, they sang another song, and the preacher began his sermon on something about "love conquering all things."

"Good grief," Brenda whispered when she found her voice. "He didn't waste a minute, did he?"

"Guess not." Molly suppressed a giggle. If it wasn't so pathetic it could actually be hilarious. Surely she was just slap-happy because of the trip; because of the fact she really thought Darrin might want to give it another try. Because somewhere down deep she was hurt beyond words, and only laughing would help.

"She's wearing your suit," Brenda whispered.

"My feller and my suit," Molly said. "Didn't leave me much today, did she? Hey, come over after services and tell me just what has happened in two weeks."

"Molly?" Darrin deliberately bumped into her after services while everyone visited on the church lawn. "I see you made it back."

"Yes, I did," she said. "What a lovely suit, Beth. Did you find yours on sale, too? I never buy anything that hasn't got a sale sticker on it."

"Of course not." Beth hugged up closer to Darrin's arm. "Some of us get what we want when it's available. We don't wait around until it's on sale," she said in a sugary sweet voice.

"Momma's got dinner nearly ready, honey." Darrin looked down into Beth's eyes like he was going to have her for lunch and maybe supper, too. "Be seein' you around, Molly."

"Sure, Darrin," she waved. *Not if I see you coming first,* she thought.

* * *

Brenda and Kayla arrived in the middle of the afternoon, just as Hilda was leaving to do volunteer work, like she did every Sunday afternoon and several evenings a week at the hospital in Sherman. "You girls better learn to whisper quieter," she scolded. "Kayla would've made less noise than you did if she'd been sittin' in church instead of going to the nursery."

"Oh, Granny." Brenda patted her shoulder. "You're just jealous because we didn't sit with you and tell you what we were talking about. I 'bout hyperventilated when Darrin and Beth made their grand entrance. Bet you did, too."

"Course I didn't." She picked up her purse. "I've been tellin' Molly for months that Darrin is no-account. He'll just sit there on that farm and let his folks support him until they're gone, and then he'll lose everything they've worked all their lives for. Especially if he keeps that fluff ball he had hanging on his arm today."

"Now, Granny, Beth is a pretty good journalist. She's been in most of my classes, and she finished last month. If I hadn't wanted to take this last crash course they offer, I would've been done, too," Molly said.

"Yep, and if you'd been done, you would've been the white suit sitting between him and his momma. Thank the good Lord above for putting you in that class." She rolled her eyes and shut the door behind her.

"Tom says Darrin told him he's really getting serious about Beth. She's going to work at the Sherman newspaper in the classifieds beginning next week, but she really wants to settle down and start a family. They could be engaged in a few weeks. I hope that doesn't break your heart. Maybe you'd like to talk to him and see if you could get things back on track." Brenda gave her pretty little blond-haired daughter a coloring book and crayons from a tote bag she brought in.

"No, thank you," Molly said.

"But you've dated Darrin for years and—"

"And I'll cut my losses and get on with life," Molly said. Kayla could have been her daughter if she would have listened to Darrin when she graduated from high school. He'd already finished two years of college, majoring in ag-business, and he wanted her to marry him right then. But she wanted to go to college, get her degree, and then she wanted her graduate degree and kept putting him off, until last December when he wrapped an engagement ring and gave it to her in front of his whole family.

"You must have already cried buckets of tears." Brenda sighed. "You don't have to put on a fake front for me. I'm your friend."

"Somehow there's no front to put on," Molly said. "I figured I'd cry myself to sleep at night, but I didn't. It's actually a bit of a relief. I don't think I ever loved Darrin. He was just there, and I'm not sure he loved me, either. Or he would have been willing to let me be me instead of changing me into a clone of his mother."

"He said some pretty mean things about you and Carson Rhodes. Said you were probably sneaking around behind his back even before you gave the ring back. Even said that you might have been playing up to the professor to get him to give you the assignment with Carson. I told him he had grits for brains, that you were talented and the professor knew it," Brenda huffed.

"He's got a right to say whatever he wants. Anyone who is my real friend will know I'm not that kind of woman," Molly said. "Let's go outside and push Kayla in the tree swing. And Brenda, don't worry about me. Strange as it may seem, there isn't even a void where he was. Like I said, I think I just went along with his plans until he made some that I couldn't abide. And I think he saw a different woman than who I really am. I'm fine. For real."

They rehashed the whole thing a few more times until suppertime, when Brenda had to leave. She'd promised her folks they'd be at their house for the evening meal, and although neither of them could understand Molly's lack of emotion or attachment to the man she was really and truly engaged to, it was time to go. Molly walked her around to the front of the white frame farmhouse and waved at Kayla until she couldn't see her anymore.

She sat down in the porch swing and kicked herself

off with one foot, then folded both her legs under her, sitting Indian-style as the hot summer breeze blew her hair across her face. She tried to analyze the feelings in her heart honestly and figure out just why Darrin hadn't affected her the way he should, but the answers just weren't there. It must have been pure fate and a whole team of guardian angels working overtime that kept her out of a loveless marriage with a man who couldn't have loved her if he wanted her to change that much.

She heard the pickup coming down the road before she actually saw it and figured Granny might have cut her hours short that evening. Then when she saw the red front end, her heart skipped a beat. Carson had brought the pictures by early instead of calling like he said he would. She was wearing cut-off jeans and a tank top, no shoes, and only the final dregs of makeup, most of which had long since been sweated off as she played with Kayla in the swing. She didn't have time to rush inside and get dressed or even freshen up, so he'd just have to take her, sweat, onion breath from lunch . . . and all.

She expected Carson to sling open the door, his dimple to indent as he smiled, maybe to be wearing his old faded work jeans and one of those white T-shirts that seemed to be his hallmark. But instead, Darrin stepped out of the truck. He shook his freshly starched jeans down around his dress boot tops, smoothed the front of his bright red shirt down behind a silver belt buckle with a bull rider on it, and eyed her for a few minutes before he walked up to the porch and hiked a hip to sit on the railing.

"New truck?" she asked as he made his way to the porch steps.

"Got it last week. Other one was two years old and I needed a new one," he said.

He looked down at her with a disgusted sneer, which fairly inflamed her angry side. Something between absolute disgust and pure hatred. "Molly?" he tilted his chin up even higher and stared down the slope of his fine-boned nose.

"In the flesh," she smarted off.

"What happened out there?" he waved his hand to take in the whole state of Texas.

"Who knows. I guess we lost the Alamo, and then the Mexicans ruled for a while." She continued to be a smart aleck and didn't even care that he treated her like she was so much trash.

"You know exactly what I mean, and you're evading the issue because I was right." He punctuated each word with a poke from his forefinger.

"I don't really care if you were right or if I was right. I don't even know if I passed the test or if I'll have to wait tables for a living after the next two weeks," she said without getting up. She wiggled one leg out from under her bottom and pushed herself off again, enjoying the soothing, rhythmic motion of the swing.

"Are you going to apologize and come back to me?" he asked.

"Only in your dreams," she said with a shake of her head.

"You owe me that much. You owe me. Five years I've waited . . ."

"I don't owe you jack squat, Darrin. It wasn't me who laid down the laws two weeks ago. I just did the job I was trained to do."

"Oh, yes, you did, and I bet you did it real well," he sneered.

"I'm not going to listen to you be ugly and hateful. Just go home, Darrin, or go get Beth for evening church services. You two look cute together, and I understand you're already talking about making her a ranch wife," she said softly.

"You were wrong," he raised his voice.

"I'm not arguing with you. It's over and I'm not apologizing for something I didn't do. Just go home, Darrin."

"I waited five years for you to finish your foolishness. Now you just tell me to go home," he said.

She'd stated her cause, voiced her opinion, and he still sat there glaring at her like he'd like to watch her go up in flames. "Darrin, next time you propose to a woman, do it romantically. Take her outside under the moon and stars and tell her you love her more than anything else in the world. Don't give her a package with an engagement ring in it in front of your whole family and say, 'Now it's official.' And then go back to watching a ball game on television."

"Now I can't even propose right," he pouted. "If I remember right, I asked you to marry me five years ago."

"Yes, you did." The swing stopped but she didn't push it again. "You said, 'Let's do a double with Tom and Brenda.' I can only remember two times in the whole five years when you said you loved me."

"Man shouldn't have to say what the woman already knows," he said gruffly. "You knew I loved you. I never cheated on you or nothing."

"Okay, then, I'm just telling you how I feel," she said. "And the strange thing is, I feel nothing. Not remorse. Not sorry. Not love. Not sadness. Surely if we'd been really in love something would be there, Darrin, and it isn't. Not even jealousy over Beth."

"I'm giving you one more chance." He stood up and brushed the seat of his jeans even though there was nothing on them.

"No, thank you," she said. "I don't want one more chance. I just want to move forward with my life. And that includes being a journalist. Going where the job is. Doing whatever I need to do."

"You just lost the best thing that will ever happen to you, Molly Baker," he said, raising his voice only a little bit. "You'll be sitting here in this two-bit farmhouse with that old Indian woman until you're as old and crazy as she is."

"Maybe so, Darrin, but I'll be happy doing it. Good-bye." She dismissed him with the wave of a hand.

He had started the ignition when the second red pickup truck roared up the driveway and pulled in beside him. Carson bailed out of the truck and grinned at her across the yard as he held up a sack full of picture envelopes. "I got them early and couldn't wait for you to at least fan through them." He noticed that the other truck's driver's window was easing down. And he was eyeball to eyeball with a big blond-haired man.

"You Carson Rhodes?" the man asked.

"Yes, I am. What can I do for you?"

"Not a thing. Just wanted to see what the next sucker looks like who she's going to leave out in the cold. And you don't look like nothing." The window started back up.

"What?" Carson drew his eyebrows down in a frown.

Molly giggled under her breath. Then she laughed out loud, and before Carson could get to the porch she was holding her sides. Darrin threw the truck into reverse and slung gravel all over the side of Carson's truck.

"What was all that about?" He sat down on the porch swing beside Molly and opened up his bag of gold.

"Darrin doesn't like my new best friend." She wiped her eyes. "Now show me the turtle on the yellow line and the ones of the cemetery. I'm buying the first calendar off the press with those pictures for my granny's friend. Oh, Carson . . ." She forgot all about her former fiancé as Carson put the first picture of the big buffalo in her hands.

"It is absolutely magnificent. He looks like he could charge and come running right out of the postcard at me," she said. "Give me more. I can't wait until tomorrow when we can spread them all out and make the words fit them. Oh, look at this one of the hawk against the sun. I told you it would be gorgeous. Bet if that company has a thing to do with *National Geographic* it'll be on the cover soon."

Carson took a deep breath. Darrin had come and gone. Evidently from what he'd said out there, it was over. That meant the field was open and he'd be hung from the nearest oak tree with a brand-new rope before he let anyone else move in on Molly Baker.

Not without a fight.

Chapter Ten

Molly set up her laptop in the library at the college in Durant, Oklahoma—Southeastern Oklahoma State University, where she and Carson both had scholarships and where Professor Johnson had taught for so long no one could remember when he wasn't at the college. A younger teacher said once that Professor Johnson set up class under the magnolia trees one day right after the big rain, the one that lasted forty days and forty nights, and they built a college around him.

Carson spread pictures over the tables. He lined them up in the order he'd taken them and put a tiny little sticker in the front right-hand corner of each shot. Molly would correlate her writing by numbers to go with each one. They would divide them into stacks according to what they had in mind when the picture

126

was taken. Calendars, postcards, tour guide information. It would probably take all day and part of the
night, but they fully well intended to have it ready by
tomorrow morning to present to Professor Johnson.
Hopefully by the end of the week, they'd know if they
had already passed the test or if they were required to
do some kind of written examination.

Carson wrinkled his brow and Molly bit her lip. He
brushed a piece of lint from the picture of the buffalo.
She slipped her disk into the slot and called up her
files.

"Well, this is it," she sighed. "The finale begins."

"It's what we worked for the whole two weeks," he
said. "What do we start with? Tell me what you wrote
down the first time."

"Oklahoma sunrise. Let's start with the sunrise calendar we had in mind. If they want to use them for
postcards for each state, I'll give them a one-liner for
that option. That one right there. Number one." She
pointed and he put the number on the sticker, then
cross-referenced it according to the negative number
on the strip and the number he'd already given that
roll of film.

"Then you think the right way to do it is categorize
the package for them?" he asked, already busy picking
up the rest of the sunrise and sunset photos from more
than a dozen states and Canada.

"Yep, make their job as easy as possible. Make ourselves indispensable," she said. "Prop them up here

and I'll find what I'd already done and we'll see what you think."

"Okay, number one, roll one, negative one . . . three one's in a row." He filled in the picture.

"Here's what I've got." She found the right place and did some fancy cutting and pasting to another file. "Think it sounds all right. Red sunrise in the land which less than a hundred years ago was Indian Territory."

"Good for the calendar. What about the postcard? This will be in every souvenir shop in the whole state, and I almost missed it. Remember, you had to point it out to me."

"I remember. Now hand me that one in Nebraska. Thank goodness we got a good sunset in New York. We could have gotten lots of rain pictures in that state. Should have taken a whole roll. Rain in the mountains. Rain over the forest. Rain drops on the WELCOME TO NEW YORK sign. Then we could have sold a calendar to folks who love being depressed and hate sunshine." She smiled and worked her magic with the next picture, number 1/2/2.

"We'll do that one when we get sent to the rain forest." He laughed, loving the way she kept using the words *our, we* and *what do you think*?

At noon they were beginning to make a small dent in the pile, and her stomach growled as it protested in hunger. "I'm starving. Why don't you go find us some crackers and a Coke?"

"Better yet, I'll go find us a couple dozen tacos at the fast food place." He picked up the picture of the place where they ate in Omaha and remembered how much she liked Mexican food.

"Sounds wonderful," she said. "I'll keep working on this last sunset. Mercy, how many different ways can a person describe a sunset?"

He waved and was gone before she looked up again. Working with him was much easier than she thought it would be. He was just as nervous about this assignment as she was, if not more so, and he didn't take any of it lightly or for granted. His future was at stake as much as hers.

"Wow, that didn't take long," she said in a few minutes without even looking up from the words forming on the monitor as she typed.

"What?" a feminine voice asked.

Molly stopped and looked up. There stood Beth Atkins in a pair of skin-tight jeans and a bright orange tank top. "Hello, Beth, what can I do for you?"

"You can stay away from Darrin. You didn't want him, so don't call him and invite him out to your place again. He told you he didn't want anything else to do with you, Molly. You made your choice when you picked Carson Rhodes over him, and you'll be sorry. Carson is a ladies' man. He might be nice to you for a while, but you haven't got what it takes to hold him any more than you could keep Darrin." Beth propped a hip up on the table where the pictures were spread out.

"Beth, this sounds like some kind of soap opera or second-graders fighting over jump ropes at recess, and I hope we're both a little more mature than that. Good luck with Darrin. I hope you are both happy. I don't think I ever loved him like I should have if I was going to marry him." Molly's blue eyes never left Beth's, and from the way the girl squirmed, it must have made her very uncomfortable.

"Well, I love him, and I've not only got your fiancé, I've also got your job. I got hired at the Sherman newspaper this week." She stood up, and four pictures fell on the floor, but she made no attempt to pick them up.

"Congratulations," Molly said. "I hope you like it. But I've got a lot of work to do, so if you'll excuse me."

"There will never be a steady paycheck in calendars and postcards, Molly Baker. You'll starve to death." Beth tossed her blond hair back and left in the same snit she arrived in, but at least she had the last word.

"But Carson just went for tacos," Molly mumbled with a short giggle. "So I won't starve today. And today is all I've got, Beth. I've no guarantee for tomorrow."

Molly's fingers were suddenly still, and no words danced on the monitor screen. In the blink of an eye, she realized what Beth had just said. Not about Darrin, but about Carson. And in that same split second, she knew she was in love with Carson and even the minute that the revelation came to her.

She leaned back in her chair and propped her feet on the table beside the computer. Now wasn't that a fine kettle of fish? How in the world could they go do a calendar of the rain forest if she was staring at him with big puppy eyes?

Oh, stop it, she chastised herself. You won't ever stare at anyone like that. And you don't have time to be worrying about falling in love right now. Besides, he's probably got a whole string of women waiting on his front lawn for him to hold out the golden scepter to. He may even have a number machine like they have in the J C Penney store. Take a number and wait until he gets bored with the one in the house and calls out the next number. And I refuse to ever be a number in anybody's book. If I can't be number one, then I really won't marry until I'm fifty.

She pulled her feet down and was deep in thought about the mountains of Pennsylvania for the tour guide when he opened the door and the aroma of tacos followed him into the room.

"Hurry up." She stood up and stretched her muscles. "Stiff and hungry," she said. "Let's put food on that table."

"Sure." He unloaded the sack on the table she pointed to, then noticed the pictures Beth had knocked off.

"What are these doing on the floor?" he demanded in a harsh voice. "Good grief, Molly, you don't knock my pictures off and then just leave them there. This is the one of the hawk you liked so well. If I'd stepped on it, we would have been another day getting our package ready," he scolded.

"Don't you talk down to me, Carson Rhodes. I'm hungry and I'm irritable, so you better watch your attitude."

"I don't care if you could eat a mountain lion, claws and all. If you knock my pictures off, then pick them up. Look. Here's my footprint and I came within a hair of stepping on it." He laid it gently back on the table.

"Don't you act like that with me." She set her jaw and wondered how in the world she ever thought for even one split second she could be in love with a man like Carson. He didn't ask her if she'd knocked the pictures off. He didn't even think that he might have done it himself before he left, or that someone else could have been in the room. Oh, nosiree, just jump to conclusions and blame her.

"Don't you treat my things disrespectfully," he shot right back as he pulled out a chair and unwrapped the paper from a taco.

I'm not going to tell him a blessed thing, she thought as she ate the first taco. I refuse to work with him on another project, as she ate the second one. He's egotistical and he talked down to me, as she devoured the third one. I hope he has to take the sportswriting job and work with Beth Atkins, as she unwrapped the fourth one.

She's mad as a wet hen, he thought as he tore the paper from the second taco. If they tell me I have to take her along to do the writing, then I'm not going on any more jobs for this company, as he chomped into the third one. All she had to do was pick them up when she knocked them off, as he picked up the fourth one.

"Beth Atkins came in here," she said through only slightly clenched teeth. "She's taking a job at the Sherman paper."

"So?" he retorted.

I won't tell him jack squat. She thought, as she reached across the table and grabbed her fifth taco and brushed his hand as he grabbed for another one. I don't care if I get the hives every time our flesh touches.

"Your old flame Darrin was in the parking lot when I got back. Beth was getting in that new truck with him and they were kissing." He baited her on purpose to see what kind of reaction she had when she heard about her ex-fiancé.

"So?" she smarted right back at him.

She's cold as a well-digger's brass belt buckle in Alaska, he thought as he turned his head to look out the window. I may just let whoever wants that sassy piece of baggage have it. Goodness knows, I couldn't live with someone as irresponsible as she is. Might as well back out of the situation right now before she ever knows how I really feel about her.

"Beth came to tell me to back off, that Darrin is hers from now on." Molly's blue eyes were flashing pure, unadulterated anger at him. He could almost feel the chill of her icy glare. "She leaned back on the table and she knocked the pictures on the floor. Then you came back in before I could even stand up and take care of it."

Carson stood up so fast he knocked the folding chair backward. It made a loud bang as it hit the floor. Molly figured he was going to storm out of the room in disbelief. Just let him. Let him go somewhere and cool off that hot temper of his, and when he got back, maybe they could get back on their purely professional level and get this package ready for tomorrow morning. She pushed her chair back and crossed the room to look out the window. Students stood in little pockets on the lawn, waiting for the next class to begin. Summer courses. So much to cram in so little space. Today was all she had, she thought again. She could turn around and finish the fight with Carson or she could pout.

She turned just in time to find him right behind her. He wrapped her into his arms, tilted her chin back, and kissed her soundly, tasting tacos and the chill of the Coke she'd been drinking. "I'm so sorry," he whispered in her ear. His very breath made goose bumps the size of mountains on her arms.

"Me, too." She cupped his face in both her small hands and pulled it back down to her mouth for another soul-searching, mind-boggling kiss.

While two hearts melded together and two halves of separate souls found their mate, Professor Johnson bounced down the hallway toward the door. He had the doorknob in his hand when he looked through the window and saw them embracing. He let go of the knob as if it was red hot and took two steps back. He chuckled and turned around three times right there in the hallway. It had worked! Put the right molecules of hydrogen and oxygen together and it made water, and even though he knew little or nothing about chemistry, he'd managed to accomplish just what he set out to do.

He eased back down the hallway a few steps and started whistling, loud and off key. When he got to the door he rattled it a few times as if it was hard to open and then burst into the room in a hyperactive manner. Just like he did everywhere he went so there wouldn't ever be a reason for Molly and Carson to think he'd been there a few minutes earlier.

"Well, my star pupils are back." He grinned, noting that Carson's lips were slightly swollen and Molly had beautiful high color in her cheeks. "Mrs. Thomas said you were in here working on putting the whole enchilada together." He fairly well danced over to the table to look at the pictures.

Molly exhaled almost audibly. If Professor Johnson hadn't been whistling, he would have caught them acting like freshmen, kissing in the hallways before class time. That would have sure made him want to recommend them for another job. He'd said they could do the work without thinking about gender. Well, it all went to show that Professor Johnson wasn't right about everything.

"Beautiful. Wonderful." He wrung his bony hands together happily. "I love it. The company is going to be happy little campers. Well, got to run. Got a one o'clock class with a bunch of freshmen. "Oh, are you finishing this today?"

"Maybe late tonight, and thank you sir," Carson said. "We hope to have it ready for you tomorrow."

"Great, that's great. The company CEO will be here tomorrow at noon. We will take you two to dinner to celebrate. Can I have the package just before noon so he can look it over all afternoon?"

"Yes, sir," Molly said.

"Good, then get on back to whatever you were doing. And I'll tell my secretary to expect you to drop the whole thing off at noon. We'll meet you at . . ." He stopped and looked at them for suggestions.

"Wherever you want." Carson said.

"Then let's eat Mexican," the professor noticed the bag on the table. "Jalapeños. Meet you there at five."

"Thank you." Molly's hands shook as she waved good-bye to him.

"Now, where were we?" Carson reached across and drew her back into his arms. "I think I was apologizing and I think I need to do some more of it."

"And I'll do some more accepting." She didn't wait for him to kiss her but tiptoed up to his level and strung a whole bevy of sweet, short kisses across his face, ending with a long, lingering one right on his mouth.

"And now that we're best friends again, we'd better get to work or else this package won't be ready at noon tomorrow." She pushed herself away from him. It was the most difficult thing she'd ever done because the phrase came back to haunt her . . . today is all I have, and I'd rather kiss Carson all day than worry with a tour booklet.

"Best friends don't kiss like that." He threw his arm around her shoulder as they went back to their work stations. "Please tell me you don't kiss Brenda like that." He nuzzled the soft skin on her neck as they walked.

"Carson!" she exclaimed.

"Did we take a step up from best friends to something better, then?" he asked. "Do you maybe like me a little bit?"

A little bit, she wanted to stomp and scream. I'm in love with you, you good-looking hunk. I've dated. I've been engaged. But I've never been in love before, and

I don't care what Beth says. I will keep you if it takes every ounce of my energy for the rest of my life. Because today is not worth having if I can't have it with you.

"I think I must like you a lot," she whispered. "And now pick up a picture and let's put off just how much I like you until this is finished. We've got to be professional right now."

"Okay." He grinned and her heart melted in a puddle at his boot tips. "I don't think I like you a lot, though. I know it."

"Give me the picture of the WELCOME TO INDIANA sign." She rolled her eyes as he handed it to her and purposely lingered until their fingers touched again.

"Carson." She shook her head at him. "We've got to work."

"Okay, okay," he sighed. "But after tomorrow night when we meet this big CEO, can I take you to dinner and forget about work for a little while?"

"Deal." She reached out to shake hands with him, and he drew her into another long, passionate kiss.

"Carson," she panted when she came up for air.

"Why do you keep pulling me away from my job, woman?" He spun around and picked up a picture.

Darrin had called her "his woman" and she'd wanted to shoot him. Carson called her "woman" in a teasing manner and all she wanted to do was kiss him again. She must really have been bitten by the old love bug.

Chapter Eleven

Molly dressed carefully in a long black straight skirt with a kick pleat up the back to her knee, a pair of black flat-soled shoes, and a plain white shirt complete with a button-down collar. The only thing with any color was the vest she chose, black denim with the state flag of Texas embroidered on the back. She picked out plain gold hoop earrings and wore her open heart necklace.

"This is it, then?" Hilda poked her head in the door and sized up her granddaughter with a critical eye. "Looks pretty uptown, but you're not going to a funeral child. You could put on some color, other than too much rouge on your cheeks."

"I don't have any blush on," Molly said.

"Well, all I've got to say is something is making

your cheeks red, and if you don't have rouge on, then by golly, it must be you thinkin' about that Carson Rhodes again. I swear, three weeks ago you couldn't stand the thought of him, and now every time I mention his name you get all jittery and red-faced. Not that I'm griping, mind you. Not one bit. Anything is a blessing after Darrin. And besides, I like Carson. Don't know why you didn't bring him around here months ago. He's intelligent, mannerly, and good-lookin' enough that if I was fifty years younger, I'd shove you out of the way and sit by him on the couch myself."

"Are you sure that's all you've got to say?" Molly teased her as she fluffed back her black hair and put her earrings in.

"Nope, but it'll probably be enough for today. Except you said you got color and all I see is black and white. Big hotshot man coming to talk to you and you don't wear nothing but black and white. Seems to me . . ."

Molly turned around and looked backward over her shoulder. "Color, see? The good old lone star itself."

"Then sit with your back to him all evening," Hilda snorted. "I'm off to see my friend Lucy. I've been telling her all about this calendar going to come out next year with pictures of old cemeteries. She says if I ever get you raised, the two of us might take a trip all across the United States and look at them."

"You'd love it, Granny," Molly said.

"Well, it's done now. The package, as you and Carson call it, has been delivered and now we'll see if it's acceptable. Good luck, sweetheart," Hilda kissed her child on the forehead. It didn't matter if Molly was her grandchild. She'd raised her and done a bang-up good job of it, too, so today she was her own just as surely as she'd given birth to her twenty-three years before.

"Thanks, Granny," Molly said. "I think I hear Carson's truck now. I'm more nervous than . . ."

". . . the only chicken at a coyote party," Hilda finished for her with a grin. "Get on out of here. If that man don't see talent as well as beauty before his eyes, then he's blind and you don't need to work for him anyway."

"Mighty beautiful tonight." Carson opened the door of the truck for her and then kissed her quickly on the lips.

Hilda was giving her a thumbs-up sign from the porch. She started to wave back to her grandmother, standing there so full of herself, but decided to give her a full show. She wrapped both arms around Carson's neck, stood on tiptoed, and really shared a kiss with him, a deep, passionate kiss like the one just before he left at two o'clock that morning when the job was finally finished.

When she opened her eyes, Hilda had both thumbs up in the air, and although Molly wasn't a mind reader, she could tell that her grandmother's feet were just barely touching the porch steps as she floated down them. Molly wondered what in the world made such a difference in Granny's attitude toward two men. Both Darrin and Carson were the same age: twenty-six. Both of them were handsome: Darrin, with his blond hair and green eyes. Carson with his sexy black hair and brown eyes.

It's because she sees with her heart. She sees past the outside and right into the core, Molly finally realized. Just the raw soul, she thought. The rest was just window dressing, which was fine to look at, nice to stand beside, but made a poor lifetime partner.

"Whatever are you thinking about so hard that it makes furrows in your pretty forehead?" Carson asked as they drove back toward Sherman.

"My granny," she said honestly without giving away too much information.

"She's not sick, is she?" he asked sincerely. He liked Hilda Baker, and hoped she lived thirty more years. Every time he and Molly came home from an assignment he wanted to eat pinto beans and cornbread and fried chicken and tell her about the trip. He'd never had so attentive an audience as Hilda was that night when they drove up to the farmhouse.

"Oh, no, she's fine. Full of spit and vinegar, and giving advice out in bushel baskets," Molly said.

"Then listen to it. She's about the wisest woman I've ever met. My grandparents have all been gone for years and years," he said.

"But you don't know what the advice is," Molly argued.

"Doesn't matter." He turned north toward Oklahoma. He'd completed two years of college while he was in the service and then finished up his bachelor's degree at Southeastern a year ago. He had enough money left by being careful and working hard all summer in the hay fields to go ahead with graduate work. And today was the culmination of all those long nights, working with headlights and moonlight.

"But what if it's about you?" she asked.

"Mrs. Baker is wiser than me and you both put together," he said. "Listen to her, even if it's something I won't like."

Professor Johnson stood up when he saw them enter the restaurant and waved them to a back table. Molly took a deep breath. The time had come and this was it. Tomorrow morning she might be wearing calluses on her knees praying for a job like Beth Atkins just landed. Or she might be down at the local cafe in Bells flipping burgers. Carson reached down and took her hand in his, and all the butterflies doing the watusi in her stomach were gone. They were a team, a professional team, and whether they swam or drowned was just the verdict right now. The sun would still come up tomorrow. There wouldn't be a blizzard in Durant, Oklahoma in the middle of July. And if that great big bear of a man who held their future in his hands didn't like what he'd read and looked at all afternoon, then next week the professional team of Baker and Rhodes just might go into freelance work.

"Molly Baker and Carson Rhodes," Professor Johnson made the introductions as Carson pulled the chair out for Molly. "This is Robert Harris, CEO of the magazine corporation I told you about. He's been holed up in my office, using my chair all afternoon and hasn't even told me what he thinks. Oh, here's our waitress." He nodded and a lady brought them menus and tall glasses of ice water.

"Are you ready to order?" the lady said.

"Yes," Professor Johnson said. "I'll have the beef enchilada dinner and Coke to drink."

"Fajitas," Mr. Harris said. "Double the order and Coke is fine. Do you bring those chips and picante to nibble on while we wait?"

"Yes, sir, and also queso," she nodded.

"Good, bring double the amount. I'm hungry. This old miser didn't even offer me a mid-afternoon snack," Harris laughed, both of his chins and chest wiggling in unison.

"I'll have chicken fajitas," Molly said. "And Coke."

"I want beef fajitas," Carson put his order in last. "And Dr Pepper, please."

"Thank you," the lady said, and with a motion a young man brought four small bowls of queso and picante and two large baskets of warm chips.

"Now, I suppose you are wondering what's on my

mind after reviewing your package all afternoon. I won't keep you waiting until after dinner, although I should send old Benny here outside. He's been pestering me for my opinion for an hour." Robert looked at the professor affectionately. "You know he was my professor, and that was thirty years ago. He's never going to retire. Someday they'll just miss him in class and find him graveyard dead in that chair of his."

Molly laughed out loud at the vision those words conjured up. "They might not even bury him in a casket. They might just lower him down in that chair."

"Oh, no." The professor rolled his eyes. "They're going to call a taxidermist and stuff me, put me in my chair, and set us both in a glass case just inside the doors of the administration building," he said, so seriously that Carson laughed.

"I don't really know just how to tell you what I thought of your work," Mr. Harris said, bringing the subject down to earth and on a serious level. "I guess maybe rather than tell you, I will show you." He loaded a chip with picante and popped it in his mouth as he opened a briefcase beside his feet.

Molly thought he'd never finish chewing that chip. She wished she could revise the rules of etiquette and make it all right to talk with food in your mouth. It seemed like he was moving in slow motion as he took a plain old spiralback notebook from his case. Just a plain red one with the green sticker from some discount store still on the front, but with the words Niagara Falls written in black magic marker on the outside.

She reached under the table for Carson's hand for the same support and "I don't care" attitude she'd lost somewhere between the front door and right then. He interlaced her fingers with his, and a silent message traveled from his own nervous heart to hers. One that said we're together in this as surely as our fingers are entwined together. Whatever he says, we are adults and we'll face it with dignity. We may fuss, fume, and even cry later, but right now we will react like the full-fledged professionals we started out to be and still are.

"I usually write down any changes I want made in the wording or whether I want to see another copy of a picture, lighter, darker, closer, farther back," he explained as he moved the chips back to give himself more room and dipped another one in queso before he let them get too far away.

Molly considered taking the basket to the kitchen and tossing every single chip in the trash can. Next time she had an assignment review, she was absolutely going to fight tooth, nail, hair, and eyeball against having it over dinner. Patience, she kept telling herself as she held on tightly to Carson's hand.

"So anyway," he wiped his mouth with the over-sized cloth napkin and laid the notebook on the table. "This is the verdict."

Molly stared at the fifty-nine-cent book like it was

a grasshopper. Right there within a foot of her hand was the verdict as he called it. Pages and pages of numbers with what changes he wanted beside them. She and Carson would be working until the wee hours for several nights if Mr. Harris had a strict deadline.

"Well, are you going to open it or not." The professor talked around a chip in his mouth, not caring one whit for manners. Anyone as old as he was could do what they wanted, anyway. If the people around him didn't like it, they'd just chalk it up to old age or senility, or maybe even both.

"I'm sorry. This is some good queso." Mr. Harris flipped open the cover to the front page.

Carson and Molly both shut their eyes at the same time, both afraid and yet scared not to look at all the changes. Neither of them were above a little constructive criticism. Goodness knows if they had been, they would have been weeded out of this profession way back when they were first beginning.

"There's nothing there," the professor said, in such a bewildered tone that Carson and Molly's eyes popped wide open and they stared at the blank sheet. "Does that mean you didn't like any of it? That you are rejecting the whole package?"

"No." Mr. Harris laughed again. "It means I held my pencil in my hand all afternoon and for the first time ever in my profession I didn't make a single mark on this book. I've filled whole books on projects before. But today I reviewed possibly the best presented package I've ever seen. I am in the position at this time to offer you both a job with my company. You'll work out of Dallas and go where we send you, bring home the goods to me."

"Whew," Molly exhaled slowly. "I can't believe it."

"Me, either." Carson let go of Molly's hand and extended it across the table to Mr. Harris. "Thank you, sir. I'd be more than glad to work for you."

"Me, too," Molly followed suit.

"But I haven't even told you the terms," the man said. "Don't jump too quickly or I might lower your salary. No, I wouldn't do that. I recognize talent when I see it, and the package I'm going to offer you is going to be good enough to keep the other sharks from enticing you away from me." He pulled a couple of envelopes from his case and handed one to Molly and an identical one to Carson.

"You take these home and study them. The salaries, the bonuses for good packages, the insurance, retirement, the whole package, and if you're agreeable, call me tomorrow at my office in Dallas and we'll set up an appointment for you to come to my office," he said. "I don't care where you live, together, apart, if you marry each other or become old misers like Benny here, I just want you standing before me within five hours of the time I call and say I've got an assignment . . ."

Molly blushed scarlet and a little bit of red appeared around Carson's ears.

"Just don't let anything get in the way of your work. This is good, and I mean really good. Have either of you ever heard of Barrow, Alaska?"

Molly shook her head immediately. Carson thought about it a moment and shook his head slowly also.

"Well, get into your computers and encyclopedias for whatever you can did up on it," he said. "It's called the top of the world, and now that you're unofficially on my payroll, it's where I intend to start you. You get to start off at the very top!" He laughed at his own joke.

Molly remembered Hilda teasing her about going to Alaska next year. Well, she was wrong. It looked like Molly was going this year, unless Robert Harris wasn't going to put them in the field until later.

"There are no roads to Barrow." He chomped a chip, and Molly let the tension ease out of her muscles, but only a little bit. "You have to fly in and out. Here's a visitor's guide I scrounged up for you this time, since we're short on preparation time. It will tell you what kind of clothing and footgear is best for your visit to the Arctic. From now on you can find your own guides."

"Yes, sir." Molly took the brochure and laid it beside the envelope, which made her hands itch to open it.

"Here's the deal," Mr. Harris said. "The bowhead whale is an arctic baleen whale and is a protected species. Not many of the big old boys left anymore. But there's a group of native Alaskan Indians up there in that part of the world who have a special permit from the important people to take one of those whales a year. They're pretty rich in blubber, I guess. The whales, not the Indians." He chuckled. "Anyway, in two weeks you are flying out of Dallas to Barrow and you're going to live there a few days, get to know the Indians and their culture a little bit before the great whale hunt, and then you're going to cover it. Start to finish."

"Thank you," Carson said.

"Don't thank me, son," the man looked across the table. "By the time you get back to Texas you'll be cussing me. You'll think you'll never be warm again and you'll want a pan of cornbread and good old Tex-Mex food so bad you'd trade your contract in on it, but unless I miss my guess, you'll bring me home a priceless package. One I can open up this book"—he tapped the notebook still beside him—"and there won't be a single pencil mark."

"We'll do our best," Molly said.

"Then it'll be perfect. I hear our food sizzling, and behold, there it is. How many sopapias are you going to eat when we finish?" he asked the professor.

"Huh," he snorted. "You eat those worthless chunks of dough. I'm having hot apple pie served with ice cream and caramel sauce."

Molly didn't care if they ate fried grasshoppers right then. She might have even gone out in the pasture and caught them barehanded for the professor and Mr. Harris. Tomorrow this was all going to sink in and she was going to float all the way up to the Pearly Gates. But right at that moment, she simply buttered a flour tortilla, loaded it with chicken, grilled bell peppers, and onions, added a dollop of guacamole, and ate with as much gusto as the three men surrounding her.

"Did we pass the test?" Molly asked when Mr. Harris had said his good-byes and was gone.

"What was the test?" Carson pushed his plate back. "Was it whether or not Mr. Harris liked the job?"

"Had nothing to do with that." Professor Johnson's tired old eyes twinkled.

"Do we still have to take something written?" Molly asked.

"No, I expect you've written plenty, and your pictures were faultless as you could see by the notebook right there." He pointed at the empty book Mr. Harris had left on the table. "You obviously have learned all I could teach you. You both get an A for this last course. You've already done your dissertation and it was approved before graduation. So this was the final thing. And you passed."

"If the job itself wasn't the test, then what was?" Molly frowned.

"The test, my children, was to see if you could work together. I never doubted your talent for a minute. If I had, I would have never recommended you for the

job. Robert Harris has only given me this kind of opportunity twice in thirty years—I wouldn't disappoint
him for anything. You were engaged to be married,
Molly, and you have to admit it wasn't an easy thing
to give that young man back his ring, was it?"

"Easier than you might think." She laughed.

"So the test was whether or not we came back alive
or whether one of us murdered the other one," Carson
smiled.

"Exactly. I knew you could do the job and all future
jobs if you could abide each other for two weeks on
an expedition like that. So the test has been passed.
And like the man said, I don't care if you marry each
other someday or what you do with your personal
life." He crossed his fingers under the table. "Just keep
on working as the best team I've ever had the privilege
of teaching. I'm going now. Papers to grade. Life to
get on with. Maybe in another twenty years another
Molly and Carson will come through my classes."

"Thank you, sir," Molly said.

"Thank you, sir," Carson stood up and shook his
hand one more time. "We'll be in touch. Goodness
only knows, we'll probably need help along the way.
And thanks for your confidence in us."

"Listen to your hearts," was all he said as he walked
to the cashier's counter and paid for dinner.

Chapter Twelve

Carson reached across the table and took both Molly's hands in his. "We did it, Molly. We really did it," he whispered.

"Even after a whole week of floating around in the clouds, I still can't believe it," she said. "Here comes our waitress." She pulled back her hands but he didn't let go.

"I'll start off with an appetizer plate of jalapeño poppers to keep me alive until the ribs get here. Then I want the dinner portion of original baby backs with the potato soup. Load up the bacon and cheese and go light on the onion. French fries and sweet tea to drink," he told the waitress, but didn't even look up at the young lady with long red hair and eyes almost as blue as Molly's.

"And you, ma'am?" The woman turned her attention to Molly. The black-haired woman didn't look like the kind who would attract the man's attention. She had nice eyes but then so did he, and mercy, the way he filled out those Wranglers and starched white shirt just about gave her a speech impediment. If someone as handsome as he was ever looked at her like that, the waitress knew she'd just swoon dead away.

"I'll have the exact same thing he's having," she said. "Little lemon in the tea, please."

"It's done, Carson." She let out a big sigh. "We signed the contracts and all the tax forms and the insurance papers and all those zeros in the salary about gives me pure old hives."

"I know," Carson nodded. "But we're a team. One of those special kinds, according to the professor. And in a couple of weeks we're off to Barrow, Alaska, to watch the great bowhead whale harvest."

"It scares the liver out of me," she said.

"We'll make it." He didn't let go of her hands until the waitress put a platter of jalapeno poppers between them. He'd asked Robert Harris to recommend a restaurant to them and even invited him along for a celebration dinner, but the man said he had another date already lined up. He shook hands with both of them, and told them their flight schedules would be ready to pick up at his office the day before they were to leave. The officials were waiting to sight the pod of whales coming up the coast, but they'd be leaving a few days before the whales made it to Barrow. After that he was already thinking about another assignment. Very different from Alaska. He was sure they'd like it.

"What's the next one, do you think?" she bit into a popper and rolled her eyes in appreciation. "Can we eat at Tony Roma's every time we come to Dallas to fly in and out?"

"It can be our ritual. Kind of like the old couple at the hotel in Springfield," he said. "And I have no idea where the next one is. I think Robert Harris likes to spring little surprises, but hey, he can surprise me for the next twenty years and then he'll be ready to retire."

"Maybe you'll have his job," she said.

"I don't want it. I don't want to sit in an office and tell everyone else to go out and do something adventurous. I want to be the one with the camera, with you beside me with your trusty old ten-cent ballpoint pen stuck in your ponytail," he said.

"Maybe it's the lost tribe in Africa," she laughed. He hadn't said he was falling in love with her as fast as she was him. Maybe he was going to be satisfied with passionate kisses and hard work.

But Molly wasn't.

Carson comfortably slipped his arms around her on the porch swing. She had a three-ring notebook filled with information they were studying by the porch light. It was well past midnight, and Hilda had long since told them that her old bones had to have rest. She wasn't as young and spry or as stupid as they were, and if they were still awake at daybreak they were in charge of breakfast.

"Bowhead whales grow to be 80 to 110 tons, Carson. I can't imagine a mammal that big. Not even with the pictures right here before me," Molly said.

"Put it away, Molly, and let's talk about us for a while instead of whales." He nuzzled his face down into her neck, breathing in the aroma of her perfume and the fresh night air.

"Okay, what about us?" She let the book fall from high enough to make a loud pop when it hit the wooden porch.

"I think you know what about us," he said. "I'm . . ." He almost said he was in love with her, but it just wouldn't come out of his mouth.

"Shhh," she put her fingers over his lips. "Don't say anything right now. Just look up there." She pointed to the sky where the moon and one star had settled into the middle of a ring of clouds.

"What?" he asked.

"It's a fairy ring," she said. "It's an omen. Brings good luck. Those are Indian fairies dancing around the moon, and anyone who sees the ring can make a wish."

"You're kidding me. What about everyone else? Do only Indians get to make a wish?" he asked, wishing that he had a tripod in the truck and some black-and-white film. But even then he didn't think he could actually capture the awesome spirit of the sight.

"Of course not. I'm sure the Irish say it's colleens dancing around the moon. And probably the Italians swear it's their fairies. I just know I've only seen two in my whole life, and they're absolutely majestic."

"As much as Niagara?"

"Nothing is that majestic. Not even a bowhead whale full of blubber for those Eskimos." She turned her face to his, wonder in her eyes, just remembering the emotions she had experienced at the top of the falls.

"Why?"

"Because it touched my soul." She looked deep into his eyes and waited for the kiss she knew was coming.

"Mine, too," he whispered as he bent forward and softly brushed his lips across hers. "Words aren't there for what it said to me. Even the pictures didn't do justice to it. But maybe between the two, it will draw people there to feel the same thing we did."

"I hope so, Carson. Everyone should see themselves once in a while like God sees them. It's something they'll never forget." She laid her head on his shoulder and made a pretty big wish on the fairy ring.

Hilda was in and out of the room so many times that morning that Molly began to wonder if she'd ever get everything in her suitcases. "Don't forget your warm socks. It's going to be cold up there, Molly." She shook her finger at her. "And take this with you."

"Thanks, Granny. I forgot it last time, but in the middle of the whale hunt I might need it." She put her mini-cassette recorder in her purse.

"You will call me when you get there just so this old woman knows you're safe and all that stuff," Hilda said.

"You're not old, and you trained me to take care of myself." Molly hugged her one more time before she shut her suitcases. "But, yes, I will call you. Our plane is leaving at seven forty-five, and we're supposed to be in Barrow at six-thirty. I'll call soon as I find a phone, I promise."

Hilda heard the truck scrunching the gravel in the driveway before Molly did. She wanted to tell her to listen to her heart again. That they were in love with each other was no secret anymore, even though Molly didn't mention that he'd said so or that she had. He looked at Molly with such a soft expression in his eyes that it made Hilda's heart hurt. But though she was ready for them to make a public declaration . . . mercy, she didn't care if she was the only one they told or if they stood on the top of the water tower and shouted it out to the whole world to hear. She just wanted Carson Rhodes to be around forever.

"Molly." He tapped lightly on the door and then let himself in the house, stopping in the living room. "Why aren't you waiting on the porch swing?"

"I love you." She hugged Hilda one more time. "Kiss me on the forehead for good luck."

"I didn't kiss you last time and you did fine," Hilda snorted, but grabbed Molly's face between her wrinkled hands and planted a kiss on her forehead.

"I know, but I took a big chance." Molly laughed. "We're coming, Carson," she called up the hallway.

"Let me help with those." He took one of the cases from her hands.

"I wasn't on the porch, because Granny had to inspect everything in my suitcases so I wouldn't get cold and catch pneumonia. She thinks just because we have to fly into Barrow there are no doctors or pharmacies," she said nervously.

"And she had to get a kiss on the forehead," Hilda told him. "When she was a little girl and had to do something big at school, she always wanted a kiss on the forehead for good luck. I don't think it had a thing to do with her talent and ability, just like it doesn't today, but she thought it did, and that's what mattered."

Carson brushed his dark hair back with his fingers and leaned forward. "Well, then, maybe I'd better have one, too. We might need it all the way at the top of the world, you know."

"Honey, I'd kiss you anytime." Hilda giggled like a schoolgirl. "Now you two get on out of here. Bring back the goods to make that fat old boy down there in Dallas just plumb drool on his shirt front. And bring me back stories to keep me up until the wee hours of the morning."

"Yes, ma'am," Carson hugged her after the kiss on his forehead. "We will, and we'll call the day before so you can have the beans and chicken all ready."

He raised the door at the back of the truck and loaded Molly's two suitcases and her case with her laptop computer in it. He opened the passenger door and kissed her quickly. When he turned around Hilda was standing on the porch with a big smile on her face as she gave him a thumbs-up sign.

He waved and crawled into the driver's side. "Well, Molly Baker, are we ready for this? Sure different than when we left out the last time just before good daylight."

"Oh, is it?" She raised a dark eyebrow and opened her blue eyes wide. "This is professional, Carson Rhodes. Purely professional. We might like each other a little better. You might even be my best friend, nowadays, but this is a job. And we are a team."

"Yes, ma'am." He turned the ignition. She might lecture him on their professional standing, but he knew from the way she felt in his arms that they were a lot more than just a good working team. He and Molly Baker were a team in every sense of the word, and someday he was going to say those three words which seemed to get stuck in his throat every time he tried to say them.

*   *   *

She held her breath when the pilot said they were ready for takeoff and the plane began to go backward. He reached across the seat and took her hand in his. "Afraid of flying?" he asked.

"Don't know, I never did it before," she said.

"Never flown?" He could hardly believe his ears. Everyone today had flown somewhere by the time they were twenty-three years old.

"No," she snapped. "Until our great adventure I'd only been in three states, remember?"

"Hey, you're nervous, but don't take it out on me." He kissed her fingertips one at a time, then opened her palm and kissed the soft flesh between her thumb and forefinger.

"Whew." She whistled softly. "You keep that up and I won't even know I'm flying."

"That's the idea," he whispered gently in her ear. "We're going to make it, Molly. Don't worry. This will be old hat by next year. We may be going to the interior of Africa next to find a lost tribe."

Her blue eyes began to twinkle. "With no grasshoppers, right?" They were in the air, floating among the clouds, and in several hours they'd be in Alaska.

"I can't promise that, but I bet there aren't many in Alaska right now," he said.

"Then we'll get this job done and then see just where Robert Harris is going to tell us to go next. Think we can make a package that won't even take one mark in the book again?"

"Honey, we're a team," he reminded her. "A professional team and a very different kind of team as well."

She remembered the wish on the fairy ring. It really was going to come true.

Chapter Thirteen

It was hard to believe they'd just left a Texas drought when they stepped out of the plane and into a four-wheel-drive cab to take them to the King Eider Inn. Molly didn't know what to expect, but what she saw superseded every single vague expectation from the brochure pictures. Snow and ice and cold, brisk wind twenty-two degrees and the cabdriver said the weatherman said they'd have more snow tonight, with possible wind gusts up to thirty-five miles per hour.

She shivered in spite of her warm sweater and leather bomber jacket. Carson put his arm around her and drew her up close. "So, where you from?" the cabdriver asked as they got into the main part of town.

"From Texas," Carson said.

"Well, what are you doing way up here all the way

from Texas? Poor place for a honeymoon, unless you're crazy," he laughed.

"We work for a magazine conglomerate and we're up here to do a job. The Eskimos are about to hunt the bowhead whale, aren't they?" Molly avoided the honeymoon issue.

"In a few days. Probably down around Atqasuk. 'Bout sixty miles southwest of here. You can go by motorboat, or I might be able to take you if the weather is fit. Got a friend who runs the boat if you want to charter it. Probably get a lot better pictures that way."

"Is there a place to stay at . . . where did you say?" Molly asked.

"Not like here. Little bitty place. Population about two hundred. Maybe two hundred fifty. Biggest portion is Inupiat Eskimos. They make some good parkas down there and ulus that can't be beat," he said.

"Ulus?" Carson questioned.

"An Eskimo knife. Good knife. Oh, and they make souvenir stuff too. Dolls, yo-yos, masks, mittens. Mostly the Eskimos make their money hunting caribou, fishing, and whaling. Got a permit from the government to take a whale a year for that tribe. Use the blubber, they call it muktuk, and oil and meat to keep them 'til the next year. Well, here's your inn. Pretty nice place," he said.

"You might get in touch with your friend. My name is Carson Rhodes and this is Molly Baker," Carson handed him the business cards Robert Harris had printed for them. "Let me write the number of our inn on the back."

"No need. I'll just tell him you're at the King Eider Inn. He'll call or come by tomorrow. You might want to take advantage of that hot tub in there tonight. Tomorrow is supposed to be blustery, so dress warm." The driver pocketed the bills Carson gave him and stuck the card in the elastic band of the visor. "Friend's name is John Mathis. Good luck. Ain't nothing like watching the Eskimos bring in a whale."

"Thank you," Carson said. "We'll look forward to visiting with your friend."

"Look," Molly pulled at his arm as she blew a steady stream of vapor in the air. "Can you really believe this?"

"Well, I've heard all my life about making it to the top of the world. But I didn't think I'd get here this fast or that it would be this cold this time of year," he said. "Let's go inside and find a cart to get all this luggage inside. Can't be good for the cameras or the computer to sit out in this, and I do believe I see a snowflake."

Molly grabbed the case with her laptop and one of his camera bags and followed him inside. There was no way she was leaving the precious equipment out in the weather a minute longer than necessary. She stopped beside him at the counter, and the lady handed them two keys for the rooms that had been reserved for several weeks. She told them their rooms were side by side. The presidential suite or the library was available if they needed it for business.

Molly opened the door and found a luxurious room with pine log furniture, a telephone (and she had to call Granny and tease her about being where snow was coming down outside), television, and VCR. "Thank goodness you didn't want to find a campground up here." She laughed as she helped drag her suitcases into the room off the dolly.

"Hey, that's an idea. Maybe they've got a four-wheel-drive thing like the cab. We could rent it and take some tents down to that place. How did he say it, Atqasuk? Even if they don't have a real campground, maybe for ten dollars each, one of the Eskimos could let us use a portion of their yard. We could rough it really good," he suggested.

"No thank you." She shuddered at the thought.

He wrapped his arms around her waist and pulled her tight against his chest for a real hug. "I've already been roughing it," he said. "It's been hours since I've held you or kissed you, Molly. That's rough on the heart." He tipped her chin back with two fingers and, just like always, soul met soul in the kiss.

"Mmm," she murmured.

"Now that I'm off the endangered species list, I'll take my things to my room. Dinner in half an hour. We could probably walk to some kind of coffee house or cafe," he suggested. "Or we could ask the nice owner of this inn just where we could go buy food and cook for ourselves, since there is a kitchenette in my room."

"Wonder why it's in your room and not mine?" she asked, snuggling down into his chest and listening to his heartbeat. Was it really doing double time or was that just her imagination?

"Probably an oversight or a practical joke Robert Harris is playing on us." He didn't make an attempt to move.

"Think we could find a market and make food? I'm really hungry, and even after I eat I might want to curl up in one of those chairs with a bag of potato chips and go over all this stuff about whales again. Mercy, I never knew there were so many regulations about hunting the creatures. At least the Eskimos can use a motorboat on this hunt. It would be something to be here for the one earlier in the year and watch them hunt in boats where they have to use oars." She talked to keep him close to her just a little longer.

"I'm going to unload my things now and phone down to the lady at the desk and ask about food." He stepped back. "Tomorrow we'll charter the boat and go to Atqasuk and have a look around."

"And I'm buying a parka," she declared. "If you won't let me snuggle up next to you, then I need a big old warm parka."

"Or some of those bright orange insulated coveralls

like we saw in the pictures," he teased right back. "Bet they'd keep you warmer than I do."

"All goes to show what you know." She pushed him out of the room and shut the door, but she could hear his chuckle all the way to the next door down the hallway.

Ice, snow, cold water, colder breezes, breathtaking scenery—she could scarcely form words to describe the mind-boggling day by the time they were back in their snug little rooms the next night. They'd eaten salmon that melted in their mouths. John Mathis was a find. A real diamond in the old coal mine. He translated when they couldn't understand the natives and steered them to the right places for bargains. Molly came home with a parka that she might never wear in Texas, but it was warm and the price had been right. Carson had taken so many pictures that she had pages and pages of notes.

"I want a sandwich and a whole bag of barbecued potato chips," she declared when she plopped down in the chair in her room. "But first, let me plug in the computer, and tell me again about those shots you got of the shoreline where the whales are migrating.

"You are a slave driver, Molly Baker," he moaned. "Make me a sandwich and kiss me awhile to revive my body and soul."

"Make your own sandwich," she taunted. "I'm not

worried about a body that looks like yours." She eyed him from his boots all the way to his dark hair, mussed up by the stocking hat he'd worn all day. "But now, about that soul, I could worry a lot about it." She sat down in his lap, wrapped her arms around his neck, and kissed him until they were both breathless.

"Enough revitalization of the soul. Now let's go fix food for our bodies." She finally pulled away and stood up. "Food is in your room. Work station is in mine. Too bad we don't have connecting doors."

"That would be a dangerous thing." He followed her out into the hallway.

"I suppose it would," she said.

The bowhead whale floated like a huge barge when it was dead. Two thousand years of training by their elders, who passed the knowledge and skills down a generation at a time, brought the huge creature in to the icy beach where the Inupiat began to harvest a year's worth of sustenance for their people. Molly watched in fascination, sometimes watching and writing at the same time, the lines running together on her paper; sometimes, watching and talking barely above a whisper into her mini-cassette player and hoping the cold didn't affect the machinery.

Carson snapped pictures as fast as she wrote. It was a far different situation from the trip for the tour booklet. The buffalo just stood there; the whale bobbed up and down in spite of it's great girth, length and weight.

Very little moved in the old cemeteries, which Robert Harris loved, but the Eskimos were everywhere at once. The hawk flying against an orange sun ball was nothing to capture when compared to the whale against a bank of white snow, gray skies and more snowflakes falling. He prayed that the mechanism in his cameras wouldn't be affected by so much snow and freezing weather.

When John Mathis took them back to Barrow, it was two tired people who climbed out of the boat and into the cab. They had spent the whole time sitting in a motorboat just watching, but they felt the tension in their muscles, and the amazing sights they'd seen were emotionally exhausting.

"There's soup in the kitchen," Carson said finally. "Something hot for the soul."

Molly nodded as she opened her door. She didn't know what she needed for her soul in all this confusion in her heart, but she didn't think soup was the answer. "Let me have thirty minutes for a hot shower and I'll be over and help get it ready." She didn't offer to give him even the slightest kiss.

She ran a hot bath while she stripped out of insulated coveralls, long underwear, and thick socks. She lowered herself down into it gradually and relished every moment of the warmth. And then she began to cry, great sobs wracking her body as she leaned forward and drew her knees up her to her chest and put her chin on them.

She was still snubbing like a child when she stepped out of the hot water, brushed the steam from the mirror above the vanity, and scolded herself. She was a professional journalist and there would be lots of jobs she didn't find so pleasant, but that should not and definitely would not affect her ability to do the job. Her eyes were red and swollen; her black hair hung in wet, limp strands. She turned her back on the woman in the mirror and wrapped a big towel around her body.

Carson fretted for fear his pictures wouldn't be as good as the last ones. He'd adjusted everything for the day—the lack of sun, the constant movement—but still he fretted. Where was Molly anyway? She said she'd be here in thirty minutes and it had been that long already. He had the soup hot, cheese as well as apples sliced and on a paper plate. He was hungry and she was in a snit. He couldn't figure out what he'd done. Once he asked her to be still when she was right at his elbow, and maybe he'd spoken too sharply, but he'd moved too quickly when she was writing and she'd shot him a look that would have frozen his ears if they hadn't already been frozen.

Then she just disappeared behind her door so fast he didn't even have time to think about kissing her. He wanted to hold her closely and tell her he loved her.

Then why haven't you told her so, he battled with himself. *She must think you're satisfied with status quo the way you've been acting.*

"You're late," he said with too much edge when he swung open his door at her gentle knock.

"So, are we on schedule?" she snapped right back.

"No, but I'm hungry." The edge was sharper.

"Then eat. I didn't tell you to wait for me. I said I'd help you fix it." She sat down at the small table for two. "So let's eat if you're starving."

Without a word, he sat down on the other side and picked up his spoon. "What is the matter with you anyway?"

"Nothing," she lied, hoping he didn't notice her swollen eyes or that she had to eat slowly to swallow the hot soup past the lump in her throat. They were the team, not just a team, but *the team.* The hand-picked one. The glory children of the next generation of good journalists. They made things come alive, made pictures talk and sing, made words string together like magic. He didn't need to know the sorrow in her heart right at that moment.

She couldn't force another bite down. She couldn't talk, and he was staring at her like he expected some kind of explanation. Tears were coming over the top of the dam, and any minute they were going to rush down her cheeks in rivers and all she could do was stare out the window at the snow falling in swirling circles.

"Molly?" The sharpness was gone from his voice and concern replaced it. Maybe she was homesick again. Maybe her feelings were really deeply hurt by his attitude in the boat.

"Carson." She got out one word before she went to pieces, great sobs wracking her body as she flung herself crossways on the end of his bed, her face buried in her hands.

"Honey, what? I'm so sorry if I hurt you." He apologized for everything in one sentence.

She shook her head. Carson hadn't done one thing to hurt her. Spoke sharply a couple of times, but then she'd done the same thing. They worked together. Every moment of every day wasn't going to be perfect, and she'd be a fool to expect that kind of enchanted life. They'd fight occasionally and disagree often, but that wasn't why Molly's heart was broken. She could let him think that and cover up the real reason she was so upset, but it wouldn't be honest, and if there was ever a future for Molly and Carson, it had to be built on a foundation of honesty.

He picked her up and carried her to the recliner in the corner, sat down with her on his lap and let her sob into his chest until she got ready to discuss whatever had brought this about. It couldn't be homesickness, because they'd only been gone a week this time. The last trip lasted two weeks, and she was almost slap-happy by the time they got home to Bells, Texas, but she didn't weep like her heart was split in two pieces.

"I . . ." she raised her head up finally and looked

into his soft, brown, caring eyes. "I am so sorry," she said.

"What have you got to be sorry for?" He couldn't believe she was apologizing for getting cross with him on the boat. Mercy, they were in a tense situation. The whale came in. It was a good hunt. The people were taking care of it.

"I . . . have . . . been . . ." and she laid her head back on his chest to draw strength. She finally got control, took a deep breath, and kissed him quickly on the lips. He tasted salt from tears and the faint flavor of canned noodle soup. "I let emotions override my professionalism. I'd understand if you couldn't even work with me again."

"Whatever are you talking about?" His eyes were just slits and his brow furrowed with wrinkles as he frowned.

"The whale. That great, gorgeous creature is dead." She looked at him. "I can write the paper, but . . ."

"You're mourning for a whale?" he asked.

"I'm sorry," she said again. "It was so magnificent. Like Niagara Falls. It was like they put dynamite in those two wonderful waterfalls and I had to watch them tumble down into nothing."

Carson suddenly understood what set her apart from all the other journalists in the classroom. Why her work was unique. She didn't just write words. They literally poured from her heart, and he hoped nothing hardened her heart to the point that she could accept anything to get the job done.

"I understand," he said simply, and kissed her forehead. "Molly Baker, I'm in love with you and have been for a while now."

"What?" she leaned back and looked at his face. What an incredible time for him to make that statement. And yet, what a perfect time. He'd just told her that he understood, not just with words but with his heart.

"I said I'm in love with you." He wanted to rush out into the hall and tell everyone at the inn that he was truly in love. "And I want you to marry me," he kissed her passionately before she had time to say another word.

"Mmm," she murmured.

"Is that yes?" he whispered.

"No, Carson, that is not yes," she whispered back, almost afraid her very words would carry through the whole inn. "But this is," and she pulled his face down for another kiss.

"Yes, I will marry you. Yes, I love you, too. Thank you for understanding my crazy emotional roller coaster of a day. I love you, too, and do you want to get married right here at the top of the world tomorrow morning or would you rather wait and have a Texas wedding?"

Chapter Fourteen

Hilda opened the door to the nursery at the small church in Bells. Two baby beds were shoved against the far wall to make room for Molly's dress hanging from a hook in the ceiling. Brenda was struggling into a girdle, and Molly was sitting in the floor, cross-legged in a pair of green plaid boxer shorts and one of Carson's chambray work shirts.

"Hi Granny. Is the church about full?" Molly asked as she rolled her eyes upward and applied mascara.

"Pretty full," Hilda nodded.

"If I never have to wear a girdle again, it'll be too soon," Brenda fussed.

"I picked out a dress that was flowing so you wouldn't have to girt yourself up like a trussed turkey

176

at Thanksgiving," Molly dabbed a little bit of blush on her cheeks and gently brushed over it.

"Thanks so much. I've got a six-week-old son and you're calling me a turkey," Brenda argued back.

"Girls, girls," Hilda chided. "If you argue and fight you can't play together."

"I can't wait until she gets big as a barn with pregnancy," Brenda pointed to her as she took her red brocade dress from the hanger and slipped it over her head. She turned every which way, checking herself in the floor-length mirror on the back of the door. "It is flattering," she said. "And you know what I'm not wearing this girdle. I'm not going to be trussed up all day and miserable." She pulled the skirt of the dress up and shimmied out of the girdle.

"Hmph," Hilda snorted. "I believe you might be growing up. Time's getting short, Molly. Wedding is at eight, and it's twenty minutes to the hour. I won't have a late bride. You'll be on time. Your make-up is fine and—"

"Is it already that time, Granny? Have you seen Carson today?" Molly stood up and unbuttoned the shirt.

"Yes, it is, and yes I have. And he's pretty nervous. His folks are all up there, except his mother and father, who are to be seated according to tradition. Nice bunch of family you're getting with this deal," Hilda said.

"Thank you," Molly smiled sweetly. "I think they are really special people. You look beautiful, Granny. Give me a kiss on the forehead before we put my veil on." She leaned forward.

"Posh," Hilda snipped, but she was beaming as she kissed her granddaughter.

Molly stepped into a straight raw silk wedding gown with a Basque waistline and a slit up the back to her knee so she could walk easily. Hilda fastened a string of pearls, mellowed into a lustrious ecru with age, around her neck. Then she set the short shoulder-length veil of illusion in the curls on top of her head.

Brenda sobbed once as she slipped the blue garter on Molly's leg. "Don't you dare start that crying stuff," Molly scolded. "I didn't cry at your wedding, and I'll be hanged if you're going to at mine."

"Oh, hush," Brenda wiped the corners of her eyes with a tissue. "Look at you. You're glowing. Carson is so good for you."

"Of course he is. We're a team," she laughed.

The ushers seated his mother and then the preacher led the two men from a side door at the front of the church. Professor Johnson wore a traditional black suit. For funerals, special occasions at the college, and weddings, he'd told Carson when he asked him to be his best man. Carson's black Western cut suit had been tailored to fit every muscle in his body, but he wasn't thinking about the suit when he waited patiently at the front of the church to finally see Molly that day.

Hilda swore it would be a traditional wedding from the moment they got home from Alaska, and Molly said she owed her that much if not a whole bushel more. Brenda stepped inside the double doors at the back of the sanctuary. She looked like a classic painting by one of the old masters in the red dress, but it seemed to Carson like she took forever getting down the aisle.

Then there they were. Hilda in her red suit, made from the same material as Brenda's dress, and Molly. Nothing else mattered then as his gaze met hers, because even though the church was full, there were no other people in the church.

The preacher said, "Who gives this woman in marriage?"

"I do. Carson I charge you to make her as happy through her whole life as you have made her these past few months." She put Molly's hand in Carson's and stood on tiptoe to give him a kiss on his forehead.

"I promise," he whispered softly.

The reception was held in the fellowship hall. The photographer's flash went off when they fed each other cake and toasted each other with some kind of sweet-tasting punch. "Bet his pictures won't be nearly as good as yours," Molly whispered as they joined his parents and Hilda in the receiving line.

"Bet Beth Atkins' writeup won't be as good as yours," he said.

"Beth is in classifieds," she reminded him.

"Be willing to bet you dollars to donuts that she has a hand in the writeup. She wouldn't ever let your writeup be as flowery and wonderful as that one of hers a few weeks ago," he teased.

"Mercy, I hope not. That was atrocious," Molly giggled.

"I don't think I've told you yet today that I love you," he said between guests' hugs and well wishes.

"No, but you just vowed to love me for all eternity," she said back. "How long do we have to stay here?"

"Until Hilda tells us we can leave," he said.

"Oh," she moaned.

"Molly," Robert Harris grabbed her in a bear hug. "I knew you kids were right for each other from the first time I saw him grab your hand in that restaurant. I'm so happy for you, and now I won't have to book two motel rooms when I send you out on assignment."

"Oh, Robert." She shook her head. "Only you would think of that."

"Give me the credit," Professor Johnson was right behind him. "I knew they belonged together from the first time I saw their work and saw him gazing across the room with those puppy dog eyes at her."

"Oh, he did, did he?" She smiled brightly. This was certainly news to her.

"Of course, he did," the professor said. "No matter

where he was, out in the hall, in class, or wherever, he never let you get out of his sight."

"Is that true, Carson?" She turned to find him blushing.

"Never give away all the secrets. Keep 'em guessing," he said.

It was after midnight when he carried her over the threshold at the hotel in Dallas. Tomorrow they were flying to an island Robert had insisted was just the place for a quiet honeymoon. Three days of bliss on a secluded island with lots of beach and only the hired help who ran his private house there. The honeymoon was his gift to the couple and his apology at the same time.

"Three days. I'm sorry it can't be a week or a month, but there's a new find at a dig in Egypt, and I need you two over there by the end of the week. I can't let the competitors get ahead of me." He laughed and all his chins quivered.

Carson shut the hotel door and locked it behind him. They had the honeymoon suite, compliments of Professor Johnson, complete with an in-room hot tub shaped like a heart, a fruit and cheese basket on the table, and a dozen fresh roses in a crystal vase on top of a big screen television. But Carson and Molly didn't see any of those things.

She kicked her shoes off in the middle of a kiss and started unbuttoning his shirt, letting her fingers touch all that soft hair on his chest. "I love you, Carson," she said simply.

"When did you know that you loved me?" he asked. "Was it in the room when you'd finally shed all the tears in the world for the bowhead whale?"

"No." She laid her head on his chest and listened to the steady rhythm of his heart. "It was when we came home from the first trip and Granny said there was food in the house. It was when I grabbed your arm and pulled you inside the house. I think then that what I wanted to do was grab your heart and pull it inside my chest and introduce it to mine."

"But you already had my heart by then," he admitted.

"I did?" she looked up into his brown eyes. "So when did you know that you loved me?"

"Molly, I loved you from the first moment you walked into Professor Johnson's classroom. I looked into your big blue eyes and got lost."

"Why didn't you say so?"

"Because you were engaged, remember?" He kissed the top of her hair and took the veil off, tossing it back on a big blue velvet chair in the corner.

"Then you loved me even before we left on the first trip?" She turned for him to unbutton the thirty-six covered buttons down the back of her dress.

"Yes, darling." He stopped his first job as her husband to kiss her neck, "I loved you . . . all the way from Texas."